Also by Caridad Piñeiro

Current Releases as Charity Pineiro

NOW AND ALWAYS June 2013 ISBN 1490362770
FAITH IN YOU July 2013 ISBN 1490412697
TORI GOT LUCKY December 2013 ISBN 1494775182
THE PERFECT MIX March 2014 1495948234

Current Releases as Caridad Pineiro

Books in The Gambling for Love Romantic Suspense Series

THE PRINCE'S GAMBLE November 2012 ISBN 9781622668007 Entangled Publishing
TO CATCH A PRINCESS August 2013 ISBN 9781622661329 Entangled Publishing

Books in THE CALLING/THE REBORN Vampire Novel Series

DIE FOR LOVE, December 2013, ASIN B00H6EFD5U Entangled Publishing
BORN TO LOVE, November 2013, ISBN 9781622663705 Entangled Publishing
TO LOVE OR SERVE, October 2013, ISBN 9781622663477Entangled Publishing
FOR LOVE OR VENGEANCE September 2013 ISBN 9781622662937 Entangled Publishing
KISSED BY A VAMPIRE (formerly ARDOR CALLS) October 2012 ISBN 9780373885589 Harlequin Nocturne

Books in The Sin Hunter Paranormal Romance Series

THE CLAIMED May 2012 ISBN 978-0446584609 Forever Grand Central Publishing
THE LOST August 2011 ISBN 978-0446584616 Forever Grand Central Publishing

VAMPIRE REBORN

Caridad Pineiro

A life alone . . . For nearly two centuries, vampire Ryder Latimer had lived alone, uncomfortable in the vampire world and unloved in the human world. Ryder had never dared hope that he'd find love in his endless existence.

Brought together . . . Fate brought FBI Agent Diana Reyes into Ryder's world and in the five years since they met, they've battled long and hard for a life together. With Ryder's love, Diana has climbed out of a dark abyss that had kept her prisoner for far too long.

A Vampire Reborn . . . It's been a month since Diana and Ryder became man and wife. A month since Ryder almost lost his life to protect his wife and their newborn child. But now something is happening in Ryder's body that is making him more human at a time when he needs to be at full vampire strength to protect his loved ones.

Will fear and doubt drive Ryder to embrace his vampire self and be reborn at the cost of his new family? Or will Diana's love battle back the darkness that threatens?

Sale of this book without a front cover may be unauthorized. If this book is coverless, it may have been reported to the publisher as "unsold or destroyed" and neither the author nor the publisher may have received payment for it.

This book is a work of fiction. Names, characters, places, and incidents are the product of the author's imagination or are used fictitiously. Any resemblance to actual events, locales, or persons, living or dead, is coincidental.

Copyright © 2014 by Caridad Piñeiro Scordato

All rights reserved. Except for use in any review, the reproduction or utilization of this work in whole or in part in any form by any electronic, mechanical or other means, now known or hereafter invented, including xerography, photocopying and recording, or in any information storage or retrieval system, is forbidden without the written permission of Caridad Piñeiro Scordato.

All rights reserved under International and Pan-American Copyright Conventions. By payment of the required fees, you have been granted the non-exclusive, non-transferable right to access and read the text of this e-book on-screen. No part of this text may be reproduced, transmitted, down-loaded, decompiled, reverse engineered, or stored in or introduced into any information storage and retrieval system, in any form or by any means, whether electronic or mechanical, now known or hereinafter invented, without the express written permission of publisher.

Visit Caridad's websites at www.caridad.com.
VAMPIRE REBORN Cover design ©2013 Sarah Hansen at Okay Creations
Manufactured in the United States of America

To my wonderful daughter, Samantha, my best friend forever.
You rock and I am totally proud of you.

Chapter 1

Ryder Latimer wiped the steam off the mirror and stared. For the first time in nearly two hundred years, his image stared back.

Granted it was barely there. Almost ghostly, but it was definitely his image. It was weird to see himself, to see how others might see him, after so long.

He gingerly rubbed his hand over his jaw and the beard there. Shifted his hand upward to drag his fingers through the longer strands of his hair.

It had been nearly a month since he'd had his ass kicked by Connall Burk, psycho vampire. Nearly a month since he'd almost died, but worse . . .

It had been nearly a month since he'd failed his family.

He had no intention of failing them again.

He pushed off the edge of the sink, wincing as his bones and muscles complained with the action. He had worked himself hard that afternoon, running through a series of martial arts drills in addition to an intense workout in the gym. Plus, he still hadn't fully healed from that beating. It was part of the reason for the beard and the longer hair. The most basic grooming hurt much like the rest of his body still ached from the damage he'd sustained and the way he had been pushing himself.

But that wasn't going to stop him from protecting his newlywed wife and newborn daughter.

My family, he thought, and smiled through the twinge in his jaw.

Charlie's mewl drifted in from the bedroom and his gut tightened with both joy and fear. Driving away the fear, he whirled from his almost spectral image and hurried out to where his wife sat in a rocker, nursing their month-old daughter.

The sight of his lover never failed to stir him.

Diana's head was down turned and her nearly seal-black hair fanned forward to hide most of her face, except the faint smile that graced her lips as she watched their daughter nurse.

At his entry, Diana met his gaze and her smile broadened, but then her exotic gold-green eyes narrowed. Her cop's eyes were way too perceptive. "Are you feeling okay?"

"Never better," he lied. He walked to her side and kneeled, still amazed by the miracle with which they'd both been blessed.

The baby's soft full cheeks moved with each suck and at a strong pull, Diana jumped a bit.

"Hungry little thing, isn't she?" he said and gently skimmed his index finger along the baby's face.

"Like her dad," Diana teased, cupped his jaw, and tenderly forced his head upward. "You're not a very good liar, you know."

Chagrined, he said, "Maybe you're just more observant than the average person."

She frowned. "You're still hurting. I don't get how that's possible."

He didn't either. He was a vampire for Christ's sake. In the past, he'd healed from a number of injuries virtually overnight. But then again, he'd never been beaten to within an inch of his life.

And he'd never fed from a slayer elder who was now also a vampire.

"I can see myself," he said and held his hand out in front of him, searching for other differences. Skimming his gaze down his naked body to examine himself before facing her again.

Diana's forehead furrowed and she looked at him as if he was losing it. "Of course, you can see yourself."

He shook his head and even that simple movement caused a throb of pain at the back of his head where Connall had smashed it into a solid brick wall during his fight with the sadistic vampire.

"No, darlin'. In the mirror. I can see myself in the mirror. Just faintly, but my image is there."

He waited for her disbelief, but instead there was only calm acceptance as she trailed her hand across his cheek and then skimmed it along the bare skin at his shoulder. "You're warmer, too. When you're not in your vampire state that is. I noticed that you were warmer the other night in bed."

He'd thought so also, but had been afraid that it was just his imagination or maybe even the changes in Diana.

Much like he'd had a taste of slayer blood, so had she in order to save her life during the birth of their daughter. Combined with his turning her, she was now a dhampir like their newborn child, and gifted with some vampire strength and healing, but also saddled with mortal limitations like aging. Albeit very slow and prolonged aging.

"Do you think it's possible that . . . I'm different? That the slayer blood did something?" he asked.

The baby squirmed and mewled again.

Diana raised Charlie to her shoulder, softly rubbed her back, and after a healthy burp, his wife shifted the baby to her other breast, where Charlie greedily latched on again and resumed her suckling. His groin tightened at the thought of how much he wanted a taste as well, but it would have to wait until his daughter had satisfied her needs.

"Do *you* feel different?" he wondered aloud, surprised that in the weeks since Charlie's birth and both their near deaths, they had never discussed it.

* * *

Do I feel different? Diana asked herself and while she considered that, she searched her husband's face for signs of any of the changes he was experiencing.

It wasn't just the longer hair and beard that changed how he looked, she thought. There was decidedly more color in his skin. Just the faintest tinge of peach instead of the formerly bloodless hue of his vampire flesh.

She traced his cheekbone with her thumb and cradled his bearded jaw carefully, mindful of his injuries and that he still had discomfort. Her olive skin contrasted with his, but her hand still looked normal. She still felt human with the same physical needs she'd had before.

Food and water.

Sex and love.

Even now desire awoke in her at the sight of his magnificent body and the intense emotions apparent in his gaze.

Nothing had changed in that short month since she'd been turned although deep inside there seemed to be a well of strength she'd never possessed before. But it wasn't just physical strength. It was emotional as well and she knew it was because of the man kneeling before her.

Her husband.

Charlie's father.

She had never imagined either of those things was possible and yet here they were. Both totally real.

"I'm stronger," she admitted and hated that his features tightened and his dark gaze clouded over with concern.

"I'm glad one of us is," he said and shot to his feet. "I need to go. I need to get some answers," he said and hurriedly dressed, yanking clothes from his drawers and the closet. Shutting himself off from her as he jerked them on and rushed from the room.

The door slammed shut, the sound as loud as a gunshot. Charlie jumped in alarm and her squalls soon filled the air.

Diana tucked her daughter tight against her shoulder and smoothed her hand up and down along the baby's body until Charlie's cries were little more than hiccoughs. With a final little stretch, Charlie quieted.

"That's it, little one. There's nothing to worry about," she crooned, but as she did so, she wondered if she wasn't trying to convince herself of that as well.

Ryder hadn't been the same the last few weeks and it wasn't just the physical changes in him.

Something besides his body had been broken that night and hadn't healed either.

In rare moments, she caught a hint of his vulnerability, of his fear, but then he would close off that part of himself. But she knew he was hurting in more ways than one.

And she didn't know what to do to help him.

A soft tiny sigh of contentment slipped from Charlie and Diana rose, walked with the baby to her office where she tucked Charlie into the bassinet beside her desk.

Although she was on maternity leave from the FBI, her boss and friend, Assistant Director in Charge Jesus Hernandez, had dropped off a file that morning for her to review. She had only just begun to read through it when she'd heard Ryder rise and head into the gym and Charlie had likewise awoken and needed attention.

The day had passed by in a blur of nursing, diaper changing, and worrying about Ryder.

Now it was time to return to what she was and to the one thing that brought stability in her life . . . her work.

Maybe once she could solve the puzzle of this crime she could somehow piece together what was happening with her husband and why the happily-ever-after seemed farther away than ever before.

Chapter 2

If there was one person on this Earth who might know what was happening, it would be slayer elder Benjamin, Ryder thought.

With the winter sun low in the horizon, he rushed out of his condo building and walked the few blocks west to Central Park. The air had a chill to it, but his thick leather jacket kept him warm as did the vampire he released so he could race along the footpaths and over to Central Park West. He passed by humans unnoticed, his image not even a blur because of his speed. Only a slight breeze brushed against the unsuspecting mortals until he finally slowed at the other side of the park where some of the city's priciest residences could be found.

He paused by the low wall surrounding the park grounds and leaned against it as he considered maybe heading to his friend Diego's home instead of Benjamin's lair.

Besides being his friend and business partner, Diego was a vampire elder and possibly as knowledgeable as Benjamin about what was happening in his body. But since Benjamin was the one who was paying the price with the Slayer Council for saving him after the beating, he figured he owed it to Benjamin to approach him first.

With another surge of vampire speed, he raced past the entrance to the celebrity-filled condo and the alley adjacent to it. The space was dark and little more than shoulder-wide, solely intended for the maintenance and service people to use for access to the building. He slipped through the entrance and past the security guard stationed in the hall just beyond the door. Rounding the corner, he eased into the stairwell and rushed to the topmost floor.

Whoever had designed the building had made it look like a castle, complete with turrets. It was in the vaulted spaces beneath those turrets, originally intended for just storage, that Benjamin had made his home after he'd been turned nearly six months earlier. His real home had been sold by the Slayer Council since they'd believed him dead. Given that Benjamin was currently on their shit list, the Council was in no rush to compensate him for all that he'd lost by their actions.

Ryder rapped his knuckles against the metal door to the storage space.

Even before Benjamin answered, the sympathetic vibrations of the blood link they shared warned him that the other man was home.

Benjamin opened the door and Ryder barreled past him.

"Why, come on in," Ben said facetiously and closed the door. "To what do I owe the pleasure of this visit?"

"I need some answers," Ryder said and walked around the area. He had never been in the space before. He only knew about it from Michaela, a dhampir friend and Slayer Council member. Although Ben had tried his best to make it homey, the space was so small and awkward that it made Ryder feel downright claustrophobic.

"How do you stand it in here?" he asked and finally just plopped himself into a beat-up bean bag chair so he wouldn't bang his head against the vaulted beams that sliced the space into even tinier sections.

Ben shrugged, walked over, and sat cross-legged before him on a rug that had seen better days, much like Ben had. His formerly handsome, almost beautiful features, had been marred during the attack that had killed him. A network of puckered ridges and lines of scars ran along Ben's temple, brow, and cheek where his brother had tried to bash his skull in. He'd let his sandy blond hair grow longer and wore it to try and cover the damage.

"It's not much, but it's home. For now. The Council and I are still at odds on where my monies have gone."

"If you need a place to stay, I've got an empty studio in my building. It's even furnished."

Ben arched a brow. "Really? That's a surprising offer."

Maybe it was, Ryder thought, but then again, this man had saved his life. Still, he wasn't about to get all best buds so quickly. "You know what they say: Keep your friends close – "

"But your enemies closer," Ben finished for him and peered at him intently with his sapphire blue gaze. "Is that how you think of me? As an enemy?"

Ryder shrugged. "Let's just say I'm undecided. But that's not why I'm here."

"Good. Let's get to the chase," Ben said and relaxed against the stone wall behind him.

"I don't really know how to start this . . . I feel different. My body still hurts from what Connall did to me."

"It was a brutal beat down," Ben said, but with enough humor in his tones that Ryder couldn't take offense. Of course, the humor didn't make it any easier to accept his failure that night.

"Yeah, it was savage and I'd be dead if not for you, so thanks. But it's not just the pain. My body is warmer and I can see myself in the mirror. Just a little, but my image is definitely there."

Ben reasoned through what he had said for a moment. "And you think it's 'cause you fed from me? That whatever slayer power is left in me somehow changed you? Made you more human?"

"Is that why vamps have such a craving for slayer blood? Why they'd love to drain one of you if given the chance?"

It was Ben's turn to shrug. "I was far gone when I pleaded with your friend Diego to turn me. So far gone that I don't think he had enough of a taste to find out. But once a slayer always a slayer, so it's possible that there was enough slayer blood left in me to multiply so that when you fed from me it made a difference somehow."

"But what about you? If you have that blood in you, do you feel more human than a vampire should?"

Benjamin hesitated as he thought about Ryder's question. Since being turned nearly six months earlier, he had had asked himself that more than once.

At first he had been as weak as a baby and if not for Ryder's friend Diego, he might have died. He'd begged Diego for his life and the vampire had obliged, although grudgingly. Like Ryder, he was a human wanna-be and not into turning humans.

Afterward, Diego had been the one to find this space for him and settle him here so he could heal. He had fed him and kept him in control when the vampire's blood lust had threatened to take over. He had helped him learn where to get the blood he needed without draining a human for it.

Or another slayer, he thought.

Raising his hand, he stared at it intently. The skin looked way paler than that of a normal human. Bringing it to the side of his face, he closed his eyes and let it rest there, waiting for the warmth that hinted at something other than undead life, but there was barely any rise in temperature. The only time he felt real heat was when he released the vampire that lurked beneath the human veneer.

Reaching deep inside, he focused on the power there, trying to decide if it was slayer or vampire energies keeping him alive, but he couldn't discern the difference. That wasn't much of a surprise, however.

Opening his eyes, he faced Ryder and took in the man's dark troubled gaze. "The slayers may not want to admit this, but there's more than one slayer journal – "

"You keep journals? Do they celebrate how you stake us or kill your own?" Ryder challenged.

Anger twisted his gut because Ryder's words hit too close to home. "We document how to be an effective slayer. The battles we've had and how we beat back the undead. It's how we prepare future generations."

"Color me confused, because it seems like you've got very few slayers left for the future."

Because he couldn't deny the observation, he shrugged. "Things are changing, Ryder. But as I was explaining, there are journals that discuss our histories and the source of slayer power. Rumor has it that some of the authors believed that the origins of our powers are not all that far removed from those that created vampire energies."

Ryder gestured between the two of them with his hand. "So you and I, not so different? I don't suppose Evangeline or the other hard ass slayers would like to hear that."

Ben nodded. "Probably not, but that doesn't explain why you feel different and I don't."

"Is there someone who might know? Who'd be willing to help us?"

Ben raised a brow again. "So it's an 'us' now, Ryder?"

The other man offered him a chagrined smile and stuck out his hand. "I guess it is, Ben. Shake on it, friend?"

He looked past the hand at the man. No, at the vampire. One who'd turned another human, even if it had been for good cause. A year ago, he wouldn't have hesitated to stake him for that. But as he'd said earlier, things were changing.

Ryder's actions had brought life to his wife and daughter. Six months earlier, Ryder's assistance had helped save his life and Michaela's.

Grabbing hold of Ryder's hand, he shook it without restraint. "Friends. So is that offer of the studio still good? I'm getting a little tired of banging my head against these arches."

Chapter 3

They packed up what few belongings Benjamin wanted to keep and headed back to Ryder's condo building.

At the entrance, Jason, the vampire door man, blocked their path and glanced uneasily at his boss and Benjamin.

"He's with us now, Jason," Ryder explained and that seemed to settle it for the other man.

Jason nodded, stepped to the side, and held open the door, but without the usual smile or pleasantries to which Ryder was accustomed. Much like it would take time for the Slayer Council to acclimate to the changes in their relationships with the undead, it might be a while before the vampires became used to having slayers in their midst. Even if Benjamin was now one of them.

Inside the lobby, Ryder inclined his head in the direction of the security department. "Follow me," he said and once they reached the office, he greeted the night watchman, another vampire who looked at Benjamin dubiously.

He introduced the slayer turned vampire and said, "He's moving into the studio just below my floor. Next to Dr. Danvers and Mr. Reyes." His ex-keeper and her husband, Diana's brother, could probably use someone strong nearby to protect them and his little niece if need be.

The watchman eyeballed Benjamin, still not thrilled at his presence. "Are you sure, Mr. Latimer? You know how their kind can be."

"He's a friend, Sam. I'll have the building manager prepare the security passes in the morning."

With that discussion concluded, Ryder showed Benjamin to the elevators, but as they waited, Ben said, "Do you always get what you want?"

Ryder shoved his hands in his pockets and pondered the question. He'd gotten Diana and their baby. He'd somehow managed to land on the Vampire Council even though he wasn't truly of an age to be considered an elder. Plus he was rich enough that there were few things he couldn't afford and his wealth just kept on growing thanks to wise investments. But he'd trade the Council and the money for the security of knowing his family would be safe.

"Not really," he admitted just as the elevator arrived.

As soon as they'd entered and Ryder pushed the button for the studio floor, Ben said, "Why do I find the 'poor me' tone in your voice a little hard to believe?"

Ryder's answer was swift and sure. "Before you were turned, you seemingly had it all, didn't you? But I bet if I'd asked you, you would have answered in much the same way."

With a resigned sigh, Benjamin confirmed it. "Yeah, I guess I would have. I didn't have the one thing I wanted."

"Michaela," Ryder said without hesitation.

Ben shook his head and laughed harshly. "Is it that obvious?"

"Definitely. I hope you'll do better to hide your feelings when she visits with Jesus," Ryder warned as the elevator stopped at their floor.

"I get it. I could never have made her as happy as she is now with your FBI friend," Ben said and followed Ryder to the studio.

At the entrance, Ryder paused and motioned to the door across the way. "That's my family in there. I'm trusting you to do the right thing by them."

"I will. Slayer, remember. It's our job to protect humans."

Ryder let him into a studio that was bigger than many multi-room apartments in New York. It was decorated in basic contemporary, a style Ryder didn't particularly care for, but which the real estate agent said was a better stage for the location. Holding up the key, he let Benjamin snag it from his fingers.

"We'll talk tomorrow about whom to approach to find out what's happening to me?" he asked.

Ben nodded. "Give me the morning to make some calls and do some research."

"That sounds like a plan. Good night," he said and hurried out the door.

Too impatient to wait for the elevator, he bolted to the stairwell and raced up the stairs, eager to be with his wife and child.

As he rushed in, he noticed the lights were on in her home office and the door was open. Her way of saying he was welcome.

Controlling the vampire inside that just wanted to rush over and take her right on her desk, he sauntered to the door and leaned on the jamb to watch her as she worked.

She was busy typing something into her computer while papers and photos were strewn over the top of her large maple workstation. Across the way, she'd tacked up more photos and made some notes on her whiteboards. The faces of at least two victims stared back at him beside pictures of the violent ways they'd met their deaths.

Even now he didn't understand how she dealt with that violence day in and out, but then again, she'd been a victim of violence herself. She understood the pain suffered by those left behind and the peace that only came when justice was served. But he also knew that for her, the pain from the death of her father was still very much alive deep inside her. It both drove her and haunted her, although in recent months, she finally seemed to be dealing with it and with the things she hadn't wanted to acknowledge.

Like that her father maybe hadn't been as perfect as she'd made him out to be.

He stepped into her office and she finally noticed him. He was surprised she hadn't sensed him from the blood connection they shared, but she had probably been totally focused on the case that Jesus had dropped off earlier in the day.

She swiveled her chair around and smiled. It was a bright unrestrained smile, filled with joy and more.

He definitely liked the more, he thought as she stood and met him halfway in the center of the room.

"I'm glad you're home," she said and rose on tiptoes to kiss him.

He wrapped his arms around her waist and hauled her close, needing the feel of her against every inch of him as he deepened the kiss. Over and over he moved his mouth against hers. He nipped her lower lip with his teeth and then soothed it with his tongue before slipping in to taste her and savor the warmth of her mouth and breath.

"Ryder," she said with a husky sigh as he reached between them and cupped her breast. Her nipple was already hard and beaded, begging for more of his touch. He rolled the tight tip between his thumb and forefinger and she moaned into his mouth and butted her hips against him.

His cock throbbed with the motion of her body inviting him to take her.

"Is Charlie – "

"Fed and fast asleep," she murmured, reached down and stroked her hand along his erection, making him shudder.

"Thank God, darlin'," he said and swept her up in his arms, not that he intended to go far.

He hurried over to the large couch at one side of her office and laid her down on it, then kneeled by her side to meet her questioning gaze.

"I can't wait," he said, slipped his hands under the edge of her maroon cashmere sweater and eased it up and over her head.

She was naked, her breasts heavy from the pregnancy, the nipples dark like sweet cherries. His mouth watered and in his gut, the heat of the vampire warned that it wanted a taste as well. His gaze darted to hers and he read what she wanted.

He wanted it also.

He bent his head and licked all around the tip of one breast and kneaded the other, tweaking and pulling her nipple into an even tighter peak.

* * *

Diana held Ryder's head to her and murmured, "God, Ryder. That feels so good."

As distant as Ryder had been at times, nothing had changed when they were together like this. The need, the satisfaction, and the link between them was still as strong.

It will always be like this, she heard in her head through the blood connection they shared.

She blasted back, *Love me, Ryder. Love me now.*

His groan vibrated through his body and into hers. She wrapped her legs around his waist, nestling the length of his erection tight to her center. He rocked his hips and gently bit the tip of her breast, sending a wave of desire rocketing through her.

She grabbed hold of his black sweater and dragged it off his body.

The warmth of his upper body registered against hers, pulling her back from the edge of need.

As she shifted away and he raised his head, his dark gaze met hers. His coffee-colored human gaze with not a hint of the neon that said the vampire was emerging.

She ran her hands all across the width of his shoulders and down to his chest, cupping his pectorals for only a moment before laying one hand above his heart. It pulsed there, vampire slow.

"It beats for you, Diana. For you and Charlie. You're my reasons for living," he said, the intensity of his emotions darkening his gaze to midnight.

"Whatever is going on, we'll handle it together, Ryder. Together like always."

"Together," he said, bent his head and kissed her again. Shifted his hips against hers, drawing her back into the passion they shared. Obliterating worry and any doubts from her mind as she let go and experienced the wonder of being with him. Shared the love in her heart with the man who had helped her crawl out of the abyss of darkness that had imprisoned her for so long.

He sucked and bit at her breasts. Caressed them before dipping his hands down to undo her jeans and haul them off her legs.

She had gone commando in anticipation of his return and his husky curse confirmed how much he liked that.

He danced a kiss down her body until he was at her center where he paused to nuzzle the trimmed curls there.

She shuddered in anticipation and he wrapped his arms around her thighs, urged them wider to nestle his big body between her legs.

"Ryder," she pleaded and dug her fingers into the longish strands of his hair. Invited him to do more.

He accepted the invitation, licking and sucking at the swollen nub at her core. Tasting all along her nether lips before returning to her clit again. Wave after wave of pleasure slammed across her body. Built ever higher as he eased one finger and then a second into her. Stroked her ever higher until passion burst across her body like fireworks in the night sky.

"Ryder," she cried out and arched her body, surrendering to the desire.

* * *

Ryder nearly came at the sight of her, lost in pleasure. Pleasure he wanted to share with her.

Somehow he managed to undo his jeans and jerked them down to free himself.

Plunging inside her, he stilled for a moment to savor the aftershocks of her release and as they ebbed, he moved, drawing in and out of her. Pushing in deep before retreating, stoking the embers of her passion again.

She arched her back and drew up her knees, deepening his penetration. Urging him on with her soft cries and the shift of her hips, meeting his every thrust.

Inside him, his own pleasure surged, but along with it came the call of the vampire. The heat of the immortal flared to life inside him, but was it dimmer than before? *Not as strong*? he wondered for only a moment as rational thought fled and the demon inside took over.

With a low growl, he drove into her, so powerfully that she cried out.

"Sorry, darlin'," he said, his voice filled with the rumble of the vampire.

"Ryder, look at me."

He met her gaze and she skimmed her index fingers across his cheek and offered a smile. "I'm okay with this."

As if to prove her point, she ran her thumb across his fangs and shock traveled through him that he had turned without noticing.

"It's okay," she urged and raised herself to kiss him, moving her lips against his mouth and fangs. Reassuring him with the soothing pass of her hands along his shoulders and then down to his hips.

"I love you. God, I love you," he said huskily and moved again, embracing her love and acceptance. Bringing them together with their shared passion until they were both on the edge, trembling and ready to tumble over together.

She shifted her hands upward and held his shoulders. Gently pulled him down, baring her neck to him. Understanding that he could only hold back the demon's needs for so long.

He met her gaze then and to his surprise, the hint of neon shimmered there. The dhampir in her was awakening to the demands of the vampire. Stunning him with the reality of just how different their world had become in just a few weeks. It relieved the always present fear that one day she would reject the vampire.

He bent his head and nuzzled the side of her neck. Inhaled deeply and savored the scent of her, so womanly and alive.

His gut tightened and the climax surged inside him, but also within her. He could feel it through the link they shared. Every beat of her heart, every shift of her body registered through him, driving his pleasure. Pleading with him for that final unity of spirit, body, and blood.

He drove his fangs through the fragile skin on her neck and sucked hard, feasting on her life's blood.

She called out his name, wrapped her arms around him, and raised her knees, drawing his hips close. Spurring him on with her caress and the mewls of pleasure as he fed.

He sucked again and her energy punched into him, filled with human, slayer, and vampire strength. It hurtled through his body, dragging him over the edge.

He pulled away and sucked in a rough breath as her release slammed into her again. Her body shook beneath his and caressed him, pulling his seed deep within. Drawing out his passion as explosion after explosion of pleasure burst through him.

"You feel amazing," he said and held her near, her body damp and shaking as the aftereffects of their lovemaking slowly fled.

"You're not so bad yourself," she said with a husky chuckle and twined her legs with his to keep him with her.

Not that he was going anywhere.

He eased onto her, savoring the lingering little aftershocks of their release. Wrapped up in her embrace, arms and legs entangled. Hearts beating against each other, hers a staccato beat against his more tardy rhythm until their breaths were steady and calm.

And until a tiny little gurgle from the bassinet became a slightly louder noise and then an impossible to ignore cry.

Ryder leaped to his feet and finally kicked off his pants and shoes. Sauntering over to the bassinet, he picked up his daughter and cradled her against his naked chest.

She quieted a little and opened her eyes. Stared at him with a green-gold gaze much like her mother's. Bold, brave, and intelligent.

He smiled. "You are beautiful, my tiny darlin'," he said and walked with her back to his wife.

Diana was sitting up against the side of the couch and as he neared, she held out her hands for the baby.

He passed Charlie to her and then sat cross-legged on the sofa beside them, watching as Diana held the baby close and nursed her. He sat back and took hold of Diana's hand. Twined his fingers with hers as he said, "You make a good mom."

"This is the easy part. I worry about how good a mom I'll be when there's something hard to handle."

"You'll handle it. I know you will," he said, having no doubts in his mind that she could deal with it. She'd handled much more complicated and difficult things in her life.

"I hope you're right," she said and squeezed his hand.

"I am," he replied and let the love enveloping them inside his heart, soothing the darkness that had been growing there for weeks, fueled by his fear and his failure.

I just hope I can be as good a dad, he thought, but held back from saying it.

Diana already had enough concerns about what was happening with him. He wasn't going to add to her worries.

Chapter 4

Benjamin accessed the Slayer Council's digital library of journals and entries with the laptop he had rebuilt from assorted machines tossed into Central Park West garbage cans. He piggybacked onto someone's unsecured Wi-Fi signal to get on the Internet.

Although the Council had yet to restore his abilities to reach the monies they had seized after his death, they had relented and given him certain network rights back. Hard asses like Evangeline, the current Council leader, and Xander, her former escort, had fought to prevent that, but calmer and more reasonable heads had won the battle.

He hoped that one of those calmer and more reasonable heads would help him make sense of the materials he found in their archives or possibly in one of the original journals that some of the Council members possessed.

He spent hours on the search, saving his notes to a secured account on the Cloud. He tried to untangle the jumble of the contrary indications in the comments of his predecessors as to the source of immortal power and how it had diverged into not only slayer and vampire energies, but into life forces that special humans had been able to tap over the ages.

While he knew of shamans and others who could use such life forces, it had never occurred to him that all of those powers somehow derived from one singular source.

Kind of like the Higgs boson 'God particle'? he wondered. He had been a scientist at one time before he could no longer deny the calling of his family's slayer obligations.

He sat back in the chair, fingers templed against his lips as he read through all his notes.

Just the tip of the iceberg, he thought and shoved away from the snazzy new desk in the studio Ryder had been so kind to offer him.

Ben didn't like charity even if his friend . . . .

He pulled up short at the thought. He wasn't quite so sure yet that Ryder was a true friend. As a slayer, he'd learned to guard himself against those who tried to enter his inner circle. Too many had latched onto him when they had seen his rising star in Council politics. Just as many had come to dislike him, maybe even hate him, because of the possibility he'd pass them and assume leadership.

Until his brother had betrayed and killed him, and a vampire had saved him.

Because of that, and because of the trust that Ryder had placed in him by asking him to guard his family, Ben would put Ryder in the friend category for the moment.

But a friend that he would have to watch closely. Ryder was a vampire, after all, and it was too tough to toss aside thirty-something years of slayer training and immediately embrace him.

It would take time to decide whether Ryder and his crew were truly friends or foes.

The sad part is, I can say the same of many of my Slayer Council members, he thought as he walked over to the windows that overlooked Central Park on one side. The windows ran the length of the building from west to east where he had views of the East River.

The morning sky showed only the faintest traces of the coming dawn, but inside him the vampire warned that the sun would soon rise and that he should seek shelter. Along with that warning came lethargy, inviting him to rest through the day so he would have strength for nighttime pursuits.

It had been a hard adjustment to become a night owl.

On his family's farm they'd always been early risers to work out in the fields and tend to the crops and livestock. But they'd also had their share of nighttime activity, keeping away the vampires brave enough to venture too close to the slayer family. His father, brother, and he had vanquished many undead vermin before the vampires had banded together and killed most of his family.

Only he and his brother had survived, tucked into a special hidey hole in the floor while his father, mother, and sisters died above them. While for days they waited until it was safe and his family's bodies rotted just feet away.

He still remembered the smell. Still recalled the sight of their blood seeping in through the floor boards and dripping down onto him and Bartholomew.

And now he was one of them. One of the undead, but not like them.

Just like Ryder and the others were not like them, he told himself, trying to justify what he was doing.

Trying to convince himself that it wasn't wrong to share the slayer secrets with a vampire. The enemy.

As the sun rose, his cell phone chirped to warn him of an incoming call.

Ryder.

He shoved away his disquiet and answered in his most neutral tone. "Guess you're an early bird."

"Hard not to be when your month-old wakes up every six hours," Ryder answered.

His stomach clenched a little at the thought that if things went south with Ryder and he was forced to stake him, there were others who might pay a price as well. A wife and child, things that vampires didn't normally have.

Before he could say anything else, Ryder plowed on. "Were you able to find out anything?"

"Not much. I searched through the journals and there were several mentions of a common font of power for all mortals. Those with more traditional beliefs would call it God. Others, like those who practice the Eastern philosophies, might call it *chi*. The power was stronger in some than others and at one time, the life forces were all one."

"All one?" Ryder asked, confusion peppering his words.

"Like all those on the Council. In the beginning, everyone was united in only one group and then one let power and envy corrupt him. He wanted more power and thought he should be the one in charge. When he failed to take control, he was banned to the darkness."

With a heavy sigh, Ryder said, "Sounds a lot like the bible story explaining how Lucifer and his angels were imprisoned in hell."

He hunched his shoulders nonchalantly. "There are lots of similarities in the origin stories from the slayer journals to those in the Bible. I think it's possible that they're somehow one and the same, but from different viewpoints. Even back then, those on the Council kept themselves apart from regular humans because of their heightened powers. It's possible they might have been seen as angels by the others."

"And the one who fell from grace? What condemned him to the darkness?"

"He murdered his brother and drank of his blood, thinking that it would make him more powerful," he said and couldn't avoid the pit of pain that formed in his gut at the thought of his own lost brother and the evil that had overtaken him. That had made him kill and hurt others in his quest for recognition.

"Hello to the first vampire, I guess," Ryder said harshly.

"That would be a good guess. If you can believe the stories that is," he replied.

"There's always a grain of truth in those accounts. A lesson to be learned. Adam and Eve. Cain and Abel. Someone or something inspired those morality tales."

Definitely morality tales, but simplified beyond belief, Ben thought. "Things aren't quite as black and white as those stories make things seem."

There was a hesitation on the line before Ryder said, "I'm glad to hear you're embracing something besides the whole vampire bad/slayer good mentality."

It would be tough for me not to, he thought and quipped, "Vampire now, remember?"

"Yeah, slayer, I remember. So if we accept that there is some truth to these origin stories, who might know more about those life energies and what they do?"

He dragged a hand through the longish strands of his hair and paced back and forth as he thought out loud. "Xander is the professor of the Council. If Evangeline has lasted as leader for this long, it's because Xander is the brains behind her brawn, but he's also incredibly devoted to her and to her vision for the Council."

"Even though she dumped him for that young stud muffin?" Ryder said.

He chuckled. "Yeah, even though he was dumped. Richard is next in line if Evangeline should fall. He's almost as knowledgeable as Xander."

"Why isn't Xander next in line?" Ryder asked.

He stopped short at Ryder's question. By all rights, Xander should be next. He was smarter and had been an elder far longer than Richard.

"He's not strong enough," he finally answered and considered that at one time, he would have been next in line. "Xander is too malleable and physically weak. There's not one Council member who would vote for him to take Evangeline's place."

Resuming his pacing, he said, "Richard is the one to approach and he has access to one of the original slayer journals. He's more likely to help us find an answer to what's happening."

"Can you arrange a meeting?"

He dipped his head uneasily, forgetting that he was on a phone. "I can try, Ryder. Even if Richard agrees to see us, there's no guarantee he'll either help or have the answers."

"I know, Ben. All I'm asking is that you try."

* * *

Although his vampire blood called on him to rest during the day, Ryder regularly fought that need in his desire to be more human. To share time with Diana the way normal couples did. He had worked at his desk in the morning, checking on his various investments, and now the two of them were in the gym, working out.

Ryder moved through the steps in the kata, Diana beside him, shifting in unison.

A left turn to face forward followed by a low block with the left hand.

A step ahead with a sharp right-handed punch.

A quick whirl and back to the front for another low block.

They glided, pushed forward and back, almost as if in a ballet.

Pivot, forward, punch, and then retreat.

An upper cut followed by a drop of the hands to the hips with another one hundred eighty degree turn and a double high block.

From the corner of his eye, he measured Diana's movements and strength since he hadn't been the only one who had almost lost his life weeks earlier.

Not that you could tell from her fluid and powerful movements. There wasn't a hint of hesitation or fragility to attest to the fact that his wife had not only been on death's door, but that she'd recently given birth. Well, almost nothing. Her warrior's body wore its lean muscled strength nicely, but the womanly curves were ever more rounded, especially her breasts.

Her command came in his head through their shared connection. *Focus.*

The warning made him stumble through the final punch and slide of the kata, but he recovered to end it gracefully.

They faced each other and bowed to acknowledge the completion of the exercise.

With the kata finished, she grinned and rolled her eyes. "Men. Show a little tit and it totally throws you off."

Reaching out, he playfully squeezed her breast and said, "Nothing little about those."

She slapped at him and he recognized the invitation in her gaze. "Think you can boss me around?" he asked.

"I know I can, remember?"

Yeah, he remembered all right. She'd beaten him more than once during their workouts, but he'd been training hard and this time, he planned on coming out on top. Literally.

"Prove it," he challenged and put his hands up in a fighting stance.

She arched a brow and her demeanor grew a tad too serious for his taste. "Are you sure?"

"If you're meaning to ask if I'm up to it – "

"Are you?" she asked, but raised her hands and braced her legs slightly apart, ready for battle.

Her words stung more than any punch she could have landed. "Don't patronize me, darlin'. I'm fit enough to protect you and Charlie."

* * *

Diana lowered her fists and examined her husband's features. The depths of his gaze revealed the onslaught of emotions with which he was struggling. Fear. Pride. Anger. They were a dangerous cocktail of emotions that could make him act rashly.

"I never said I didn't trust you to protect us, Ryder." If anything, her fear was that he'd do anything, including sacrificing himself, to keep them safe.

He likewise eased out of fight mode and stood there, arms dangling loosely at his sides. His shoulders slightly slumped, as if in defeat. "You don't need to say it, darlin'. I can see it in your eyes. The worry. The doubt."

She shook her head and slashed her hands through the air. "Not because I doubt that you can keep us safe, but because I worry that you'd fight to the death to do it. We've traveled down too long a road to have our journey end here, Ryder. To have it end with you dead because you let all those emotions churning in your gut drown out common sense."

He recoiled as if slapped and she instantly regretted her words. But better they be out there and discussed than festering between them.

"Is that what you think? That I'm being irrational? Thoughtless?" he almost shouted and held his hands out as if pleading for her understanding.

She grasped his hands in hers and twined her fingers with his. "I think that something really bad happened to you and it's tough to deal with that. I know. I've been dealing with something like that almost all of my life. You helped me understand what I was feeling about my father's death. I want to help you deal with this, Ryder."

For a moment she thought she might have reached him, but then he withdrew, both physically and emotionally.

"I've got to go. I promised Benjamin I'd meet him to talk over some information he gathered."

"Do you want me to go with? I can get Melissa – "

"No," he said and wagged his head forcefully, wincing slightly as he did so. "This is something I've got to do on my own. Please try to understand that."

"Okay. I'll be waiting for you," she said, biting back her concern at what he might do with the slayer turned vampire.

"I may be late. Don't wait up. You need your rest." He leaned close, brushed a quick kiss across her cheek, and bolted in a blast of vampire speed from their gym.

Be safe, she called out mentally and waited, but if he'd heard, he was intent on ignoring her.

So not good, she thought, and headed to the body bag in one corner of the space.

Beating the crap out of it was a sure way to battle the frustration she was feeling.

But the little voice of the demon inside her said beating the crap out of him would have been much more satisfying.

Chapter 5

Ryder hadn't expected Richard to be much different than the rest of the slayers on the Council.

Like the others, he refused to meet them in his super-secret slayer residence. Instead, they had to meet in one of the areas beneath the stage in the theater at Lincoln Center.

The ballet company had just finished a series of performances and was now getting ready for the annual holiday run for the *Nutcracker*. Most of the company, stage hands, and assorted musicians had already left for the night, but the sounds of activity on the stage above them filtered down to where they stood to warn them others were still present.

"You're asking a great deal of me, Benjamin," Richard said. He wore a white lab jacket from a nearby hospital, but he had removed any name tags or badges which might have revealed his human identity. He eyeballed Ryder directly, scrutinizing him the way he might some kind of specimen, and brushed back his leonine mane of salt and pepper hair.

"I'm asking that you help prove a belief that some slayers have had for millennia: that the source of our power and that of the vampires comes from one place."

And could return someone to that same place. A very human place, Ryder thought. Not that he was eager to go there. If anything, he needed to remain a vampire in order to safeguard his family.

Richard wagged his head emphatically. "I don't think I can do that."

"Can't or *won't*?" Ben pressed.

With a negligent shrug, Richard said, "What difference does it make?"

Something snapped inside him. He surged forward and jabbed a finger into the slayer's chest in emphasis. "It makes a difference to me and mine, and to Benjamin. If something is happening in our bodies, we need to know. The Slayer Council needs to know if we can be human or slayer again."

Richard shoved Ryder away with a blast of power so shocking, Ryder's knees weakened. The charge of slayer strength sizzled through his body, stinging like a jellyfish's revenge.

"Feel that, vampire? You'll never be human again," Richard said, an ugly sneer on his face.

Fuck diplomacy, Ryder thought and launched himself at the slayer, transforming into his vamp self in mid-air.

He hammered the slayer with his body, sending them both tumbling into a pile of wires and cables. The tangle of wires ensnared the slayer as Ryder pinned him to the ground, straddled the other man, and rained a shower of blows into the other man's face before the slayer could mount any defense.

He was about to land another punishing punch when Benjamin snared his hand and with a violent pull, jerked him away from Richard.

Ryder whirled to battle him and found that Ben had morphed into vamp mode also. His cerulean blue gaze now bore the bright neon-green of the vampire and his fangs, shorter than Ryder's thanks to his newly turned state, were visible past the edge of his upper lip.

"This is not the way," Ben said, the warning growl of the vampire alive in his voice.

The slither and clank of metal against cement drew their attention to Richard, who was liberating himself from the mess that had trapped him. Ugly bruises marred one cheek and his jaw, and blood leaked profusely from the corner of his mouth.

"I was willing to accept that the Council needed a new way to work with the vampires and dhampirs, but now I ask myself,

'Why?'" Richard said and wiped away the blood with an angry swipe of his hand.

"Why? Because you're dying out, slayer. You kill your own, but call us monsters," Ryder said. He laid a hand on his chest to make a point. "Inside there's a heart that knows how to love. That wants to protect his family."

Richard scoffed. "Family? Your dhampir wife and child? You should have let them die, Ryder. All you've done is condemn them to a life of isolation and pain."

The man's words hurt more than his blast of slayer power, maybe because in his gut, Ryder recognized the truth of them. Whether dhampir or vampire, they had to live their lives apart from others. *Alone as I had been for so long*, he thought, but then reeled himself back from that thought.

He was no longer alone. He hadn't been alone in a long time.

Pulling his shoulders back and raising his chin at a stubborn angle, he glared at Richard. "I'm not alone. *We're* not alone," he said and gestured between him and Ben.

Richard laughed and shook his head. "Wanna-bes. When push comes to shove, you'll show your true nature, like you did just seconds ago. Inside you're foul and full of malevolence. In time that evil will win out and it won't be pretty when it happens."

Ryder glanced at Ben whose tight features revealed his anger. "It's time to go, Ben. If this is the most reasonable elder on the Slayer Council, I pity them."

With a nod, Ben sadly said, "I do, too."

The two men hurried from the area, leaving Richard to go his own way, probably back to the hospital to finish his shift.

They morphed back into human mode as they hit the street outside the theater. Ryder sucked in a deep breath of the winter air to tame the heat of the vampire and the lingering bite of the slayer's charge along his nerve endings.

"That went well. Not," Ben said from beside him and jerked up the collar of his jacket against the chill air.

Ryder shook his head. "No, it didn't, and I'm sorry. I shouldn't have lost my temper, but his arrogance was too much too handle. You slayers obviously get a healthy dose of that during your training."

"Yeah, we do," the younger man said with a chuckle and a shake of his head of shaggy sandy-colored hair. But his tone turned serious as he said, "Death sucks it out of you, though, you know."

Yeah, he did know. He had thought himself all brave and noble until he lay dying on a Civil War battlefield, the victim of a vicious vampire attack. At that moment, he'd have made a bargain with the devil for just another second of life and yet when he'd gotten his wish, he hadn't felt relief at first, only anger.

Anger like that which still burned in his gut from the encounter with Richard and needed to be quenched before he returned home.

He tilted his head in the direction of downtown. "I'm going to blow off some steam. Are you game?"

Ben's bright blue gaze widened in surprise. "You want me to come with?"

He shrugged. "A pint at the Blood Bank might be helpful."

"No, thanks. I'm still not into the drinking in public thing, but I'll head down with you. I thought I might pop in on Michaela."

And Jesus would just love that, Ryder thought, and just in case, he said, "You might want to give her some warning."

With a nod, Ben whipped out his smartphone and sent a quick text. He shoved the phone back into his pocket and said, "Ready to fly?"

"Whenever you – "

He didn't get a chance to finish as Ben disappeared in a blur of vamp speed.

Ryder whirled and chased after him, dodging past the pedestrians on the street and in and out of traffic until they were in the high twenties where the buildings weren't as tall. There they shot up to the rooftops, leaping from one to the other. Seemingly flying until they reached the end of the Flatiron District and dropped down onto Union Square.

Michaela and Jesus lived in one of the condo towers just to the south of the square. The Blood Bank was even farther downtown on the Lower East Side.

With a brotherly clasp of Ben's hand, he moved away from the other man, but tracked his journey as he sauntered over to the tall condo building, his head buried in his phone as he walked. He wondered if Michaela had texted him back and if so, what she'd said.

Jesus didn't seem like the kind of man who'd take too kindly to her former lover hanging around a lot.

But Ben kept on walking in the direction of the building, so Ryder took off for the Blood Bank.

The vampire club was located in a small alley where only braver humans dared to venture. Well, either brave or out for trouble since the vampire club was regularly the source of some kind of violence. Except that things had gotten slightly better since a reformed and decidedly kinder Foley had taken over ownership.

At the mouth of the alleyway, he paused to look at the entrance to the bar. It was early so there was no line, only the bouncer whose main job was keeping the vampires from premature snacking on the patrons waiting to get in. Not that Foley was concerned with damage to the humans. It was more about making sure that the vampires had to pay for their drinks inside rather than getting them for free.

Ryder ambled to the door and nodded at the bouncer who returned the unspoken greeting and stepped aside to let him pass.

He swept past some humans lingering by the front door. They were dressed mostly in black leather with enough piercings and tattoos to send the clear message they were not to be fucked with.

Pushing on to the bar, it was close to empty and he was glad for it. He just wanted to enjoy a nice quiet drink on his own and consider all that had happened with the slayer. A great deal of his anger had already subsided thanks to the rush through the night. There was something about expending all that energy that always helped to tame the vampire and its baser emotions.

Emotions that Richard had said would one day overwhelm, only Ryder knew control was possible contrary to what the slayer had said. He regretted that he had lost control tonight and vowed not to make that mistake again.

He plopped down onto a stool and leaned back against the wall, his gaze drifting over the patrons and sizing them up. Feeling out the other undead and the strength of their life forces. Mostly fledglings for which he was grateful, although they could be bitey if they hadn't learned to control their blood hunger. No older vamps who might be itching for a fight over their territory.

"Well, lookie here. If it isn't my good friend, Ryder. How are you and the missus?" Foley asked as he stepped over to him, wiped down the scarred counter of the bar, and placed a cocktail napkin there.

"We're just dandy," he replied, but the bite was evident in his tones.

Foley grasped the towel in his hands and leaned on the edge of the bar. "Not having problems, are we?"

"Wouldn't you be glad if we were, but no, we're not. Just some other stuff going on."

"Yeah, I forget you're a big man on campus now. On the Vampire Council. Friends with the slayers," Foley said and then reached behind him for a bottle. He waggled it in question and Ryder nodded.

With a flourish, Foley whipped a shot glass from beneath the bar and filled it with thick black-cherry colored blood from the bottle. "Drink up. It's good for whatever ails you."

He snagged the glass off the counter, tossed it back, and grimaced. "Christ, Foley. It's still fucking warm."

"Only the best for my friends. Paid a fortune so the lady would make the donation," he said and then poured himself a shot which he savored more slowly. "Delicious, but I suspect you have something much more tasty waiting at home for you."

He should probably be pissed that the club owner was still Jonesing after his wife, but he knew Foley would risk his life for her and Charlie. "You know, Daniel," he said, using the given name that only true friends knew and were allowed to mention. "One of these days I may finally get sick of you having a hard on for my wife."

Foley just laughed and nodded. "Yeah, I get it. I need to find myself a girl, but the kind that comes in here is not the kind you'd bring home to mom."

"You need to get out more," Ryder said and motioned for another pour.

"Vampire, remember? But enough about me. I can tell you've got a load on your mind." He prepared another round of shots for them and after they both drank them down, relaxed against the counter to listen.

He stared hard at Foley, wondering how much to say. At one time, Daniel had been kind of a selfish hard-ass, but in the last few years, he'd redeemed himself and had demonstrated his friendship and loyalty on more than one occasion. Because of that, he faced the other vampire, leaned forward and unloaded, spilling his guts about what he thought was happening and his run-in with Richard.

"Slayer prick," Foley said and poured yet another round.

Ryder hesitated, but then picked up the shot glass. Without knowing if slayer blood was causing any changes and with slayer blood running through his wife's veins, he was going to have to practice a little abstinence.

"Abstinence?" Foley said with a hoot of laughter. "You've got that delicious treat in your bed and – "

Ryder socked him hard, rocking Foley's head back from the force of the blow. If he hadn't been a vampire, he'd likely have knocked him out, but Foley only smiled and flashed a hint of fang past the welt growing on his lip.

"I warned you," he said.

"Yeah, you did. It's actually nice to see a little bit of spirit. You've been kind of mopey since the whole Connall thing."

He should have been pissed. Should have maybe punched him again, but unfortunately Foley was right just as Diana was right about how he was behaving. Maybe it was well past time that he became a big enough man to admit it.

Reaching into his pocket, he tossed a few bills on the counter to pay for the drinks, but Foley waved him off.

"No need, Ryder. I owe you and Diana way more than that. Say hello for me. Give her a wet kiss – "

Ryder socked him again, but Foley only smiled and said, "Now that's the way a vamp should behave. All fight and fang."

Ryder shook his head and laughed. "I'll try to keep that in mind, Daniel."

Chapter 6

After Ryder had split off to head to the Blood Bank, Benjamin had hesitated for a long time before finally going to Michaela's. Especially since she hadn't answered his original text message and it had taken a second one plus a phone call for her to respond.

She'd sounded a bit distracted and he had wondered why, but as she opened the door to the condo where she was now living with her FBI lover, he finally understood that he'd come at a bad time.

A very bad time.

Michaela was in a silky maroon robe that draped her lithe body. The very feminine garment surprised him since she was normally a jeans and black leather kind of girl. Her face was pleasantly flushed, her hair sexily tousled. The fine fabric of the robe emphasized every curve and was so short, it exposed lots and lots of the creamy skin on her smoothly muscled legs.

She looked absolutely fabulous.

Not a good thought to have as her hulking lover came to stand directly behind her, bare-chested and clearly pissed off at the intrusion.

He held his hands up in surrender. "I'm sorry. I can tell this isn't a good time for a visit."

"Can you say awkward much?" Michaela said with a roll of her eyes, but waved her arm to invite him in.

He eyeballed the other man, who shrugged and possessively wrapped an arm around Michaela's waist as they stepped aside to let him enter.

He walked in, but didn't take a seat. He was clearly interrupting something and it was best he get it over with, but Michaela beat him to the punch.

"You said you had something important to discuss," she said.

"I'm going to call for a meeting of the Council and I need you to back me up," he blurted out.

"And this couldn't wait because?" she asked as she and Jesus sat next to each other on the couch.

"It involves Ryder and Diana. They're your friends, right?"

Michaela and Jesus shared an uneasy glance. "Yes, they are. Good friends and they've been through a lot lately," Jesus replied.

"We need information and the Council may have it. I went to Richard, but he refused to help."

Michaela made a face. "He's usually the most reasonable."

"But he wasn't this time. So will you back me up?"

She nodded without hesitation. "Of course."

He shifted from foot to foot, well aware that his reason for coming here was done and yet not all that anxious to leave. The studio Ryder had loaned him had every creature comfort known to man except one: Someone to share it with, but as he glanced between Michaela and Jesus, he understood she could no longer be the one. He'd be overstaying his welcome if he lingered. "I guess I should go."

His two friends shot to their feet, but Michaela laid a hand on Jesus's bare chest and said, "Could you give us a moment?"

Jesus shot him a warning glare, but then acquiesced. "I'll be waiting." As if to drive the point home, he bent and kissed her hard before heading out of the room.

Michaela faced him, tightened the belt on her robe, and then wrapped her arms around herself defensively. "You know I'll always have your back, Ben."

Oh, Lord. The Friend Zone speech was fast approaching. "I know, Mikey, and I understand it's over between us."

"I'm not saying that you're not welcome, I just need a little more warning, unless the apocalypse is here. If it is, feel free to message me."

He chuckled as she had intended. Mikey had always been able to make him laugh. Mikey had always been able to make him feel as if the battle was worth it, which made him wonder why it was that they'd drifted apart.

"Don't, Ben. Don't wonder. It wasn't meant to be," she said, clearly aware of where his brain had gone.

"Are you happy?" he asked and cringed at the cliché.

She smiled indulgently, slipped her arm through his, and walked him to the door. She paused there, cradled his cheek, and said, "Never happier. It's time for you to find someone who makes you happy, too."

After a quick and slightly awkward embrace, he stepped out. As the door closed, he leaned against the wall outside the apartment and thought, *I already did.*

* * *

It had been a long and tiring night, Richard thought as he let himself into his apartment in the 9th Avenue highrise. Besides the unsettling meeting with Benjamin and his new vampire friend, the hospital ER had been swamped. *Considering how many assault and shooting victims had been wheeled through the door, it had to be a full moon*, he thought as he walked toward the dry bar just off the foyer.

As he did so, he noticed the bright beams of light coming in through the wall of windows and illuminating one half of the room while casting the other part in deep darkness.

Definitely a full moon, he thought as he poured himself a bourbon, and glanced across the water to the lights of New Jersey and the Palisades. But as he did so, he finally sensed another presence in the dark.

He whirled and peered toward the far side of the room. Someone stood there, just beyond the light, features hidden by the gloom, but it was a familiar silhouette.

"What are you doing here?"

"You have something I want."

Richard shook his head. "I don't think there's anything for us to discuss. How did you get in?"

Sparks flared and a second later, pain erupted in his chest as the barbs dug in and electricity pumped throughout him.

His body failed him for a moment, the drink falling from his useless hand, but then he recovered and with an uncoordinated swipe, ripped the Taser's barbs from his chest. He sucked in a breath to gather his strength, but had barely recovered when another Taser round hit him. A second later hard hands grabbed hold of his arms and delivered an even more punishing charge of energy that forced him to his knees.

He would have fallen if those hands hadn't kept him upright.

His heartbeat stuttered as those hands dug in and pulled at his life energy, yanking it from him the way a knitter pulled string from a ball of yarn. Each little tug taking more and more away from the skein of his life force.

Ancient words from a dark art filled the night as his assailant murmured a ritual forbidden long ago. The words wrapped around him, tightening and strengthening the bond. Allowing his attacker to reach deeper and deeper into his life energies and continue his feeding until there was almost nothing left.

Richard's gaze wavered as he tried to focus it on the familiar face. A face now contorted by evil and hate. He hissed one final word, "Why?"

As the hands released him and he fell to his knees, nearly dead, he heard, "Because I can."

He mouthed a "No" only a moment before something sharp ripped apart his throat and spilled his last bit of life.

Chapter 7

Fight and fang, Foley had said and the words echoed through Ryder's brain along with Richard's condemnation.

Foul. Isolation. Pain.

As Ryder dropped from the rooftop onto First Avenue, each step he took toward home pounded those words into his brain. Stoked both fear and anger inside of him as he thought of his family and what he wouldn't do to protect them.

He'd do anything, much as Diana had worried. If that made him a monster, then so be it. For too long he had denied the demon that lived inside of him and maybe now it was time to embrace it and the power that it brought.

Funny thing really, he thought as he passed by a shop window and the barest hint of reflection taunted him. Just when he was ready to embrace his vampire, humanity had decided to call. But he'd fight it with fist and fang and every ounce of heart he had inside of him for his wife and child.

At the condo building, he nodded in greeting to Jason, who opened the door for him.

He was tempted to race up the stairs in vamp mode, eager to be with her again, but he held back as he noticed several humans by the elevator bank. Containing his restlessness, he waited with them, got on the elevator, and endured the multiple stops until he was at his floor. Then there was no holding back his rush home.

Through their connection, he sensed the peace within her and in a burst of speed, he raced to their bedroom.

Charlotte was in the bassinet, fast asleep. The sound of running water came from the master bathroom and he reined in his impatience and sauntered to the door. He stood there, leaning against the jamb as he watched her in the shower.

She had her hands braced against the wall and water sluiced down her body as steam billowed from the top edge of the glass stall. As she stood there, she turned her head and smiled sexily.

What are you waiting for? she said in his head and he needed no additional invite.

With each step he took across the room he whipped off another piece of clothing until he was at the door to the shower, totally nude and totally ready to make love with her again.

She turned and held her arms out to him and he stepped into the warmth of her embrace, made even warmer by the heat of the water shooting at them from all the shower jets.

"I missed you," she said and eagerly answered his kiss, opening her mouth to him. Giving as good as she got until they were both shaking and needed more.

He bent his head and nipped at her breasts, sucking and licking them as she encircled him with a soapy hand and stroked him. Cupped him with her other hand and caressed his balls.

"Oh, God," he said, his breath exploding from his body at the feel of her hands on him.

"My turn," she said and pushed him toward the shower wall.

He leaned back and the water spilled down his body, washing away the soap which was just as well since she kneeled and took him into her mouth. Sucked him hard and then teased the sensitive edge of his dick while she worked his balls until they were tight with his need.

He cradled her breasts and caressed her, wanting her to have pleasure as well. Her soft gasp of pleasure against his cock as he tweaked her nipples nearly undid him, but he held back and watched her. His body shook from the sight of her going down on him and feel of her mouth and hands, striving to please him.

But he wanted to come inside her. Wanted to be one with her when she came.

"Diana," he said and she rose slowly, pressing every inch of her body to his.

"I want, too, Ryder," she said and stroked him again.

He groaned and gently took hold of her hips. Shifted until he was behind her and her hands were braced on the shower wall, waiting for his penetration. He dipped down and guided himself to her center. Drove in slowly, savoring the friction of her body against every inch of him. When he was buried to the hilt, he waited, prolonging the pleasure of her and their union. Feeling her contract around him and grow warmer. Wet from desire.

"Ryder," she pleaded and ground her hips against him.

He moved then, pulling out and then driving back in. Reaching up and around her to caress her breasts as he took up a rhythm, his thrusts growing ever faster and more erratic as they neared the edge of release.

Her body trembled against him and she grabbed at his thigh with one hand while holding herself upright with the other against the wall. He braced a hand beside hers and wrapped his arm around her waist, supporting her as her release swept over her, weakening her knees. Rolling over his body and pulling at the demon inside him to come out and play, but he forced that back.

He'd already fed from her that day and he needed to stay human now. He needed to have control until he knew more about what was happening inside him and what her dhampir slayer blood might do to him.

Those thoughts pulled him back from the edge of his own release and try as he might to recover that pleasure, it failed him.

He grunted his disgust and stroked a few final times, prolonging her climax until she relaxed in his arms and he slipped out of her.

* * *

Diana eyed Ryder warily, wondering about what had cooled his passion. She searched his features and met his dark hooded gaze.

"Ryder, talk to me," she said, but her husband shook his head, sending droplets flying off his soaked locks.

"We should dry off," he said, averting her scrutiny as he reached behind her to shut off the water and quickly stepped out of the stall.

She followed him and he handed her a towel. That was when she noticed the abrasions along his knuckles. She grabbed hold of his hand and gingerly ran her finger across the reddened skin. "What happened?"

"Lost my temper. I guess you'd call it an altercation." He rubbed the towel across his sculpted chest and she noticed the pinkened skin on both his biceps, like hand prints on his flesh.

"Looks like someone got their licks in as well," she said and motioned to the marks.

Ryder tracked her gaze and cursed under his breath. "I guess you could say that."

"That's a lot of guesses there, Ryder. Why don't you make my life easier and tell me what happened," she said, but he did an about face, tossed his towel into the hamper, and marched out of the bathroom.

She wondered if he was intentionally trying to push her buttons or if he was truly so caught up in his own darkness that he didn't realize the distance he was creating between them.

Counting to five, because she didn't think she could really muster the patience to hit ten, she walked back into the bedroom, her pace measured and unhurried. Her stance as relaxed as she could make it to avoid escalating the situation.

He was in bed, cuddling Charlie against his naked chest.

Damn if her heart didn't do a major flip flop at the sight of him with their daughter.

She walked to his side and sat on the edge of the bed, her thigh pressed to his. She leaned forward and skimmed her hand across Charlie's head before reaching up and brushing back the wet locks of his dark hair so she could see his face.

"She was fussing," he offered in explanation and the baby squirmed a bit in his embrace, but then quieted again.

"She probably just needs to be changed," she replied, but then gently steered the conversation back to what had to be discussed. "Charlie's going to be just like a human child for awhile. She'll need both of us to be just like every day parents."

"Do you really think that's possible?" he said, his gaze still fixed on their daughter. Holding her tenderly in his large hands which made her look so so small and fragile.

"I'm trying to make it possible, Ryder. I'm trying to be a mom and do my job. Be your wife – "

"Are you saying I'm not doing the same? That I'm not trying?" he shot back, his voice growing louder which caused Charlie to fidget against him.

She laid a hand on his arm and rubbed it up and down across the faint outline of the hand print. Beneath her palm, she registered a weird vibration of power. "This tells me that you're not sharing something with me. Something that could make a difference with us. With our family."

He finally met her gaze directly and calmly said, "Ben and I went to Richard for his help. He refused and I lost my temper. He zapped me with some weird ass slayer power so I beat the crap out of him. Then I went for a drink and Foley pissed me off. So I gave him a shot or two while we shared a glass."

She narrowed her gaze and examined him. Convinced that he was telling the truth, she tried to lighten the moment. "Foley probably got off on it. He likes the pain, you know."

"He's still into you, which is why I popped him. Twice," he said with a satisfied smile and a chuckle.

Diana shook her head. "Poor Daniel. We're going to have to find him a girl of his own."

Ryder's smile broadened and he reached out, wrapped a hand around the back of her neck and tenderly urged her close. "Yeah, we are, because you're my girl, right?"

She was surprised at the hint of doubt in his tones, so she sought to reassure him. She rested her arm along his where their baby was cradled and said, "I'm yours, Ryder. Heart and soul. Brain and bone and muscle and sinew. There isn't a part of me that isn't yours, my love."

The subtle tension in his body evaporated like morning dew and he released a heartfelt sigh. He tucked her tighter and they lay together in silence for long moments, peace surrounding them. The kind of peace they didn't have in their lives often enough.

A peace that was shattered by the vibration of her cellphone against the wood of the nightstand.

Diana snagged the phone before the noise could wake Charlie. Annoyance flared in her that Jesus would be calling at such a late hour, especially since she was officially on maternity leave. She knew that eventually she'd spend her share of nights over a dead body, but not yet. Not until she'd been able to gather up a lot more moments like the one that had just passed to remind her of why she did what she did.

So that others might know peace as well.

As she glanced at the screen, she realized it wasn't Jesus calling, but Michaela.

At this time of night it could only mean one thing.

Major otherworld trouble.

Chapter 8

Ryder stood hand-in-hand beside his wife, who had had refused to let him come alone. Despite the late hour, they had taken Charlie down to his ex-keeper Melissa Danvers and Diana's brother Sebastian, Melissa's husband. He would have preferred not to have Diana here either, facing possible danger. He wanted Charlie to have at least one of her parents to watch her grow.

His gut clenched at those thoughts and he risked a glance at the others who flanked his wife. To his left were Michaela and Jesus. Both were outfitted with enough weapons and gun power to hopefully make someone think twice about starting a fight that night. To Diana's right, Benjamin stood uneasily, clad in black leather and chains. Along one arm he sported a vambrace filled with an assortment of knives. A telltale bulge beneath one armpit hinted at the fact he might be packing a gun as well.

Across from them stood most of what was left of the Slayer Council. Evangeline with her new boy toy second-in-command Anthony. Evangeline's ex-lover and ex-second-in-command,

Xander. Two other lesser Slayers whose names he couldn't recall, mostly because they tended to stay silent and kowtow to Evangeline.

Missing from the mix: Richard.

His absence created an even more uneasy feeling in his gut.

At either side of the five Slayers were half-a-dozen slayers-in-training. He could tell they weren't full slayers from the lack of power he sensed in them. In fact, he sensed no unique energies from at least four of them which meant they were truly novitiates to the slayer fold, untouched by even a scintilla of immortal power.

Each of them wore an assortment of weapons, mostly medieval in nature, although Anthony, like Benjamin, appeared to have a more modern weapon of some sort.

About time they got with the program, Ryder thought. It wasn't easy to fight either mortals or immortals in this day and age without some kind of firepower.

"Why did you call us here, Evangeline?" Benjamin said.

"Richard is dead," she replied, no hint of emotion on her face or in her tones, although her hand tightened noticeably on the hilt of the immense sword at her side.

Every inch of his body tensed and he turned his head to glance in Diana and Benjamin's direction. His wife looked up at him, before quickly peeking at Benjamin and then swinging her gaze to the head Slayer.

"How and when, Evangeline?" Diana asked.

Evangeline laughed harshly. "Why not ask your *husband*," she said with a sneer and then quickly added, "or your new friend Benjamin. They were the last to see him alive."

"He was alive when we left him," he said and Benjamin seconded it.

"He was alive. Have you spoken to his colleagues at the hospital? With his lover?"

"His lover was the one who found him, his throat slashed open. His body drained of blood."

"So he was home? Clearly alive well after Ryder and Benjamin met with him," Diana challenged.

"You don't deny they met with him then?" Evangeline pressed and looked back and forth between Anthony and Xander. Evangeline's ex seemed uncomfortable and Ryder wondered why, but he didn't have time to think about it further and delay an answer. He'd seen Diana interrogate possible suspects often enough to know delay was a sign of deception.

"We met with Richard at Lincoln Center. It didn't go well. In fact, Richard and I fought," he admitted.

"Then there's no question that you had a reason to want him dead," Xander said confidently, much as he might have when he had been second-in-command.

"He does me no good dead."

Xander turned his attention to Benjamin. "And you, Ben? All torn up that Richard's gone? He took over your spot on the Council."

Disconcertingly, Ben chuckled and shook his head. "Anything that leaves people like you and Evangeline in charge worries me, Xander."

Anthony took an aggressive step forward, but Evangeline laid a hand on his arm and stayed him.

"Let's admit it, Ben. You hate us as much as we hate you. This truce between us," Evangeline said and gestured between the two groups with her hand, "is one none of us wants, but all of us have to live with."

"We didn't break the truce," Ryder said.

"And yet one of us is dead and drained. How do you explain that?" the head slayer shot back.

"We can't, but we can help you figure out what happened. Find out who did it and why," Diana replied.

Her boss and friend, Jesus, added "We can help bring them to justice."

Evangeline laughed harshly again and jabbed a finger at each of them to emphasize her point. "You and you and you. All of you? You expect me to believe a word you say?"

"The same could be said of you, Evangeline," Michaela finally chimed in. She'd been abnormally silent for someone who was usually quick-tempered and in a rush to fight. This was more true to form, but then she continued in a more measured and cautious tone. "As much as we both might hate it, we're stuck with each other. You keep the vampires under control and we help keep you in existence."

"You're right that we hate it, Michaela. We hate that half-breeds like you and Benjamin stain the Council with your undead blood."

"But you have no choice. If you don't trust us, what about other FBI agents?" Diana asked.

"You want to expose our secrets to others?" Evangeline challenged.

Diana glanced past him to Jesus, who nodded in seeming agreement. "The agents we have in mind have secrets of their own to keep. They'll guard your skeletons well," Diana advised.

"You cannot trust them," Anthony urged.

To Ryder's surprise, another of the slayers, one of the usually silent ones, said, "What choice do we have? If Richard's death poses a threat to the Council, we *must* act."

"Silence," Evangeline barked.

"What will it be?" he said and faced Evangeline directly, tired of the discussions and worried that despite them, Benjamin and he were still the most likely suspects in Richard's death.

"Do not think that because we agree to this, you are off the hook, vampire," Evangeline replied.

"Not for a moment, slayer."

He gripped Diana's hand tightly and she said, "I'm assuming you've sealed off Richard's home."

"We have. Michaela and Anthony can take you there and after, make arrangements with us so we may attend to his disposal," the head slayer said.

Disposal, he thought. So clinical and inhumane a word from a person supposedly dedicated to maintaining humanity.

"Are you okay with that?" he asked his dhampir friend, not wanting to assume Michaela was on board with their plans.

"I'm game, Ryder." After a quick look at her lover, who nodded his agreement, Michael said, "J, too. We need to get this solved before it creates even more friction on the Council."

He dipped his head, understanding that Benjamin and she were only reluctantly allowed in the Council ranks. Michaela because she had earned her spot and Benjamin because he had been one of them before being turned.

He glanced at his wife and saw nothing but determination on her features. "Are you ready, darlin'?"

"I'm ready. We'll call Sanchez and Alexander and ask them to meet us there."

"That's the plan. Let's go."

* * *

It won't be the first time or the last that I spend a long night with a dead body, Diana thought. She paused for a moment to silently add, "or an undead one."

For now, Ryder, Benjamin, and Michaela stood guard in the hallway outside Richard's apartment. Plus, it was best to keep Ryder and Benjamin out of the crime scene to avoid any inference that they had tampered with it.

Anthony angrily paced back and forth by the door as Sanchez, Alexander, Jesus, and she took in the scene and prepared to gather evidence.

As murder scenes went, it was routine. In fact, she'd seen far worse.

Richard lay sprawled on his back, his throat ripped open. The arterial spray from the wound stained part of one wall and a nearby leather couch. A goodly amount of blood had soaked into the beige carpet beneath his body, which made her question Evangeline's statement that he had been drained.

"No signs of forced entry," Special Agent Miguel Sanchez said.

"Not at this entrance, but slayers always have an escape route in case of attack," Jesus advised and turned to Anthony. "Do you know where it is?"

The Council member hesitated since such secrets were usually closely guarded, only Richard wasn't going to be escaping to anywhere.

Anthony gestured toward a far door and what appeared to be a bedroom. "In there. I can show you."

As the most senior of the field agents, Diana took control. "Jesus and Miguel go with. Helene and I will start processing this area."

The two men followed Anthony from the room and Diana handed Helene latex gloves so they could gather evidence.

Diana yanked the gloves on and walked to where Richard lay. She faced Helene and gestured to the highball glass on the floor. Beneath the metallic scent of blood lingered the odor of alcohol. Bourbon, she guessed. The aroma was familiar as it was Ryder's preferred human libation.

"He had the time to pour himself a drink, so he either wasn't aware that someone was here with him or he knew his attacker."

"Wait a moment," Helene said, reached behind her and snapped off the lights.

Moonlight bathed the area where Diana stood. Helene was visible thanks to the light spilling in from the bedroom door. But as the men returned from that area, she called out to them, "Please shut that door."

When they did, the entire area was plunged into darkness and only their vague silhouettes were visible.

"You can hit the lights," Diana said and when they all stood together by the door, she continued. "The killer may have already been in the room, waiting for Richard in the dark. Since he didn't force the lock, he either had the key – "

"Or he came in through Richard's escape route," Jesus finished.

"Who would know about the entrance?" she asked the slayer.

Anthony clenched his jaw and answered past gritted teeth. "Another Council member."

Which meant that Benjamin and even Michaela might be suspect. For that matter, Ryder if the Council suspected that he and Benjamin had acted together. She was certain the Council would jump on the chance to eliminate Benjamin and Michaela or for that matter, Ryder. By all rights they should have sanctioned her husband for turning her, but the intercession of their Council members had made it impossible.

She jerked her head in a go ahead gesture and said, "Let's start processing the scene."

Miguel and Jesus took photos of the area, dusted assorted spots for prints, and searched for any fibers that might give them a clue while Helene and Diana examined the body.

"The throat wound is consistent with a vampire attack," Helene said as the two of them crouched by the body, examining the ragged flesh and muscle. The attack was so vicious that Richard's head was nearly sliced off his body.

Diana shook her head. "This is overkill, Helene. It was more about settling a score than feeding."

"But someone fed from him. There's not enough blood in the area for a wound this bad."

Diana scoped out the blood pool and spatter. "Or he was dead or close to it when his throat was ripped open."

"Perp was right-handed based on the path of the wound. Slightly taller from the up to down motion of the slice. He used a Taser to subdue him," she said and gestured to the marks left behind by the barbs and electrical charges.

Helene nodded. "He got hit twice by Taser blasts."

Diana examined the twin scorch spots on his shirt and then leaned close Helene. She whispered so Anthony couldn't hear. "Can you see anything out of the ordinary?"

Helene closed her eyes and a second later, a bright aura surrounded her body for a split second before Helene jerked out of that state. "Very weird."

"Weird even for an immortal? You've probably seen more weird than anyone," Diana said.

Helene, who was actually Nemesis, the Greek goddess of Justice, nodded. "There's a very unusual energy signature in the air. Almost . . . primordial."

"Primordial? So we're dealing with something other than human?" she asked.

Helene shook her head. "No, actually something very human. But also vampire and slayer."

Diana's gut tightened as she recalled Ryder's words from earlier that night about Richard zapping him. Was that the energy Helene sensed or was it something else?

"Can you get another read off him? TOD or any images?" she asked. One of Helene's immortal powers was the ability to see things by touching objects or people, but only if a short time had elapsed since death had claimed them.

Helene once again closed her eyes and laid a hand on Richard's arm. As before, only the briefest hint of aura limned her body before she shook her head. "This is so odd. I'm not getting anything at all, but he hasn't been dead long. No more than an hour or two which means I should be able to see something."

"But you can't?"

Helene shook her head. "It's almost like his brain was zapped clean. Like a computer hard disk that's been wiped by some kind of magnet or jolt of power."

Back to that zap, Diana thought uneasily. "Let's check his liver temp so we can better gauge the TOD."

Diana pushed to her feet and walked to where Anthony waited by the door as Helene worked by Richard's body. She took the measurement as Diana asked and then called out, "He's been dead for about an hour and a half."

Ryder had only been with me for the last hour, she thought.

She faced Anthony. "We're almost done here. We'll have a report for you by the morning."

"Need time to coordinate your stories? Create some alibis?" the slayer shot back.

"Let's settle this right now, slayer," she said, opened the door and asked the others to enter.

As they did, her gaze skipped over each of their faces as she asked, "Where were you at approximately eleven tonight?"

Michaela's gaze swung to Jesus and she said, "In bed with J. He can vouch for me."

"I can," her boss and friend confirmed.

She peered at Benjamin who shrugged nonchalantly. "Home alone. Your doorman or security tapes can probably confirm when I arrived at the building."

That left just one, but the most important one as far as she was concerned.

"Ryder?"

"I was in transit from the Blood Bank to our home," he answered without hesitation, although he, too, recognized that he had just jumped to Number One on the list of suspects.

"Did anyone see you? Do you remember the route you took?" she pressed, grasping at anything that might help her clear her husband.

"No one. As for the route . . . ." He shook his head and sighed. "Who knows."

"I will have to report this to the Council," Anthony replied, almost gleefully.

"We're far from finished with our investigations," Jesus advised and he was backed up by the murmured comments of Helene and Miguel. "We'd like to do an autopsy."

Anthony shook his head. "No can do. No one besides another slayer can handle him."

"How do you propose we finish our investigations then?"

"Not my problem," Anthony replied smugly and crossed his arms over his chest.

Diana sidled close to Ryder and tucked her hand into his, but he pulled away and she could feel him shutting her out through the connection they shared.

Anthony continued after a quick glance at all of them. "We'll expect concrete proof of his innocence."

"You'll get it," she advised and hoped she wouldn't be wrong.

"Then you'd best get to work," Anthony said and stood there, vigilant as they completed the few tasks they could.

Chapter 9

Ryder stood at the wall of windows, staring out at the night sky and the ever present activity along the Queensboro Bridge and up and down the city streets.

In the living room behind him, Diana and her law enforcement types tossed out scenario after scenario and reviewed the evidence they had so far. Not that they had much. Just a few scattered fibers as well as blood samples and photos of the scene. The Taser marks on Richard's body. Still, he'd seen his wife solve a crime with far less to go on.

He felt useless just standing there. As useless as he'd felt the night Connall Burk had beat him to within an inch of his undead life. As useless as he'd felt earlier that night when Richard had jolted him.

Just like someone had electrocuted Richard. After hearing Helene's comments, he had no doubt that it wasn't just Tasers that had jolted Richard.

Had the hit of energy been powerful enough to kill him or had he survived long enough to feel the bite of whatever had torn his throat open?

From the corner of his eye, he caught Benjamin's approach, but he was in no mood for company.

"This isn't a good time, Ben." His voice had the low rumble of the vampire as anger and worry ate at his control.

"There never is such a thing as a good time, Ryder. Can you remember anywhere you went after you left the Blood Bank?"

He nodded. "I've been mentally piecing together the trip home. I'm pretty sure of where I came down to street level. Maybe there's a traffic camera or some other CCTV that caught me on the way."

Like the storefront where he had seen his reflection. He could confirm it with a quick trip down the avenue, but first, there was something else that had been bothering him.

He approached Diana and her colleagues. As he neared, they quieted and looked up at him.

"Did you remember something?" his wife asked.

"Lots of little things that could maybe help," he said. "There might be video of me nearby that can confirm where I was at the time of the murder. And we had set up security cams at Foley's, so maybe there's video there as well."

"We can check on the public cameras at the office," Miguel advised and Ryder provided them information on the locations where he had been on the street before arriving at the apartment.

"I'll check with Foley," she said.

He stuttered a protest, but his wife said, "We can't let a suspect secure his own evidence, Ryder. Please understand."

He did understand, but he wasn't happy about accepting it. "I get it, Di. I may not like it, but I get it."

She offered him a reassuring smile and said, "That's a good start. Anything else?"

He dipped his head. "You felt some weird kind of power from when Richard touched me. Helene sensed something unusual with Richard."

"You want to know if it's the same kind of energy?" Helene asked and when he nodded, she rose, stood before him, and released her goddess powers. A beautiful blue aura slowly leaked from her until she was bathed in color. She closed her eyes, raised her hands, and let them hover close to his body. He could feel the peaceful kiss of her aura as she read his life force.

"I sense it. Energy besides your own," she said. "But it's different than what I picked up around Richard. Actually, the more that I think about it, it was like Richard's life force was just wiped away."

"What do you mean 'wiped away'?" Michaela asked.

"Empty," Helene said and peered at Michaela. "I can see your life force all around you. Similar to Richard's and to the lingering energy that's staining Ryder's power." She looked from Michaela to Benjamin. "You have almost none of that life force left, Ben. There's another aura of power in you. Undead energies."

Helene finally examined Diana. She motioned between her and Michaela. "The two of you have similar energies. More like Ryder's."

"What do you mean, 'more like mine'?" he asked, wondering why the goddess wouldn't group him with someone like Benjamin, who was more vampire than slayer apparently.

Helene stepped away from him and ran her gaze up and down his body. "Your life forces are mixed. Very mixed, almost like there's a battle going on inside your body."

No shit, he thought. It was much like the war going on inside his head, now more than ever.

"So what you're saying is that someone didn't just drain some of Richard's blood. They drained his life force?"

Helene nodded.

"So we've got an energy vampire at work?" asked Miguel, her partner and lover. He walked to her side and laid his hands on her shoulders protectively and Ryder understood. If someone was after intense powers, Helene was like catnip.

Diana rose from the couch and paced back and forth for a moment before facing Helene. "Could you identify if someone had Richard's power inside them?"

The other woman shook her head of curly auburn hair. "It's not that specific for me. Not like those of you with undead blood who can connect to each other through the link of that shared blood. All I can tell you is whether someone has that same kind of energy within them."

"It's a start at least," Diana said with a sigh. Facing the group that he'd come to think of as their posse, she said, "I think it's time we called it a night. We can pull tapes and get the videos in the morning. Try to alibi Ryder and figure out who on the Council might want Richard dead."

"I'll ask around about that," Michaela said.

Benjamin seconded her response. "There are still some who might speak to me about the internal conflicts."

Diana turned her attention to Jesus. "Do you think we can ask Maggie to work with some of the physical evidence? Maybe have David assist her?" she said, referring to two other members of their otherworld group of friends.

Jesus nodded. "I'll speak to them first thing in the morning."

Feeling as useless as tits on a bull, he asked, "And what about me? What am I supposed to do? Just stand here and look pretty?"

His wife winced and dragged a hand through her hair in frustration. "We'll need your help, Ryder. For right now, you need to lay low."

Fury rose up inside him, driven by that feeling of helplessness and failure that had been dogging him for over a month. "You expect me to tuck my tail between my legs – "

"Not now, Ryder," she said with an angry slash of her hand. "This is between the two of us."

"And I think it's time we all left," Jesus said and literally pushed the others out the door, leaving the two of them glaring at each other.

His body vibrated with anger, the demon clawing to be released, and he didn't fight it anymore. With a rough growl, he let him out and stalked toward his wife in full vamp mode.

"Do you actually expect me to just hide? Keep my head tucked under the covers so the slayers won't find me?" he yelled and thumped his chest with his fist.

She walked straight up to him, tilted her chin defiantly high and said, "I expect you to stop acting like a *mindless* vampire. It's what got you into this mess in the first place."

It might have hurt less if she'd kicked him in the balls. At least that pain would have eventually gone away.

He held his hands out to his sides and with a harsh laugh said, "What happened with being okay with the vamp? Because that's what I am, darlin'. What I've been since the day we first met. What I'll be 'til the day someone drives a stake through my heart. Oh, wait. You just did."

He whirled away from her and stalked a few steps back, his long strides eating up the distance to the windows.

Diana stared at his back, at the way he sucked in a huge breath and held it before expelling it harshly.

He was fighting for control. The control that had evaded him earlier that night. Twice.

Although she'd blamed the vampire, in the back of her mind came the fear that it hadn't just been the vampire out-of-control. Even in his human state, Ryder had been different lately.

Different in a way she understood because she had been that way at one time.

After her father's murder before her very eyes, she'd not only been wounded physically, but emotionally. It had taken her a very long time, years and years, for her to recover. To climb out of the abyss of darkness that had threatened to destroy her.

Darkness like that which had held Ryder for centuries until the two of them had somehow found each other. Found that love could help them climb out of the chasm of loneliness and despair.

She walked to him and laid a gentling hand on his back and like a wild animal experiencing its first human touch, he flinched before calming.

That flinch hurt more than a physical punch, but she pushed back that hurt because she needed to be strong right now. For both of them.

"All I'm trying to do is to protect our family, just like you. I can't do that alone, Ryder. I need you at my side. I need you."

His head dropped forward as he said, "I know, darlin'. I know. It's what I want as well."

"So we'll do this like a family, right?"

He nodded, but somehow she didn't feel reassured. Especially when he didn't turn, but stayed there, staring out at the darkness.

She stepped back and said, "I'm going to the Blood Bank to round up whatever video Foley has. I'll be back."

"I'll be here," he said, but as she marched away, she wasn't so sure *her* Ryder would be there when she got back.

Chapter 10

Benjamin, Michaela, and Jesus stood in the cold night outside Diana and Ryder's condo building.

Jesus looked up toward the penthouse and Benjamin knew where his thoughts lay. With their friends who were clearly suffering.

"I don't plan on waiting until morning to hit up the other slayers," Benjamin said.

"How soon before they take Richard's body away?" Jesus asked.

"They're probably doing it as we speak," Ben said.

"Any way to get another look at the body?" Jesus asked.

"Maybe. I know where they take the bodies to be cremated," Ben replied and at that Jesus looked toward Michaela.

"Will you both go there and try to hold up the cremation while I call Maggie and David? There may be other evidence we'll lose if they make him toast."

Michaela nodded. "We can do that, J. We'll call once we're there to let you know if were successful."

Jesus glanced at Helene and Miguel. "I know it's late, but could you head into the office and check those video feeds? Try to confirm Ryder's whereabouts, but also check the feeds around Richard's apartment building? We might luck out and find something hinky going on."

Helene and Miguel hurried off and Ben was about to go with Michaela when Diana came charging out of the building, every line of her body vibrating with anger.

"Here come's trouble," he muttered under his breath and the three of them waited until she approached.

"I thought you guys were going home for some rest?" Diana said and eyeballed her three friends.

"I thought you were going to call it a night?" Michaela challenged in a way that only Michaela could.

With a harsh chuckle and a shake of her head, Diana nodded. "Yeah, I did, only I'm too wound up to rest. I need some closure on this, at least with respect to Ryder's involvement. I'd lay odds on the fact that no matter what we find out tonight, this is going to be a much longer haul."

"I agree," Jesus said. "Anthony said only slayers can touch Richard, so Ben and Michaela are going to try and intercept Richard's body to get some more evidence."

"Thanks," she said and glanced at them. "Ryder had marks on his arms where Richard grabbed him. Maybe whoever drained Richard left similar hand prints," she said and ran her hands along her own arms to emphasize her point.

"We'll get photos if they're there," Michaela said.

"Try to put something in the photo to show scale. A dime or penny will do," Diana advised and turned her attention to Jesus.

"Are you running this op?"

"I think that makes sense for now. I've sent Helene and Miguel back to headquarters to review videos. Since you're here, how about the two of us go to the Blood Bank to see what Foley may have?"

"That was my plan," she said. "I just hadn't planned on having company."

"Always good to have backup, Di. My car's around the corner," he said and motioned toward First Avenue. Bending slightly, he skimmed quick kiss across Michaela's cheek in an obvious sign of possession. She returned the kiss before she and Ben glanced at one another and then took off in a blast of vamp speed.

"I don't think I'll ever get used to that," Jesus said with a wag of his head.

"There's lots of things I don't think I'll ever get used to," she said and took off at a hurried clip toward his car, feeling a chill that only had a little bit to do with the winter's night.

Jesus had remote-started the sedan, so heat blew from the car's vents. Diana slipped into the passenger seat and turned a number of them in her direction, hoping to chase away both the cold and her disquiet.

Her boss and friend took the wheel and drove off, making a series of turns to get them going south and toward the Lower East Side. Despite the late night hour, there were still a good number of vehicles along the city streets, but not enough to slow them down as they rushed to reach the Blood Bank.

For the first few minutes, Jesus said nothing, although she could tell he was itching to ask. But he knew her well enough to know that she wasn't going to talk until she was good and ready. The thing was, she needed to talk. Needed to get her worries out there where she could maybe make sense of them.

"We had a fight," she said and watched his reaction from the corner of her eye.

He shrugged. "Couples fight. Hell, Michaela and I have had our share of disagreements."

She had no doubt that he had, understanding the dhampir slayer all too well because in some ways, they were a lot alike. "It's not easy loving someone who's headstrong," she said and risked a glance at her friend.

He shifted his gaze from the road for a second before acknowledging her statement with a nod. "It's not easy, but it's worthwhile. But I suspect we should be talking more about him than you."

She shrugged, uneasy about sharing her fears, almost as if she was somehow betraying Ryder, but Jesus would keep her counsel. She had no doubt about that.

"He's changed in the past month. Ever since everything that went down, he's been different. Distant."

"Dangerous," Jesus added, his hands clenching on the wheel, almost as if he was bracing for her response.

But she couldn't deny what he'd said. "Yeah, there's that. It's like he's losing control. Losing himself to his dark side," she said and nervously rubbed her hands up and down her thighs.

"He was already there when you first met him, Di. Somehow you managed to reach him."

Yeah, I had, she thought. The man she had first come to know and fall in love with had been dark, dangerous, and so alone. So much like she had been at that time. She had often wondered in the years since then if they hadn't been brought together to bring balance to their lives. To bring them light, security, and love.

She reached up to the gold crucifix she had started wearing again months earlier and clutched it in her hand. She'd told herself time and time again as she prayed for Charlie to be born alive and healthy, that she had to have faith.

She told herself that again. Reminded herself of the darkness into which she'd slipped after her father's death when she'd lost faith in so many things. God. Justice. Even her family.

Sucking in a deep breath, she said, "I don't know whether I reached him or he reached me, Jesus. But I was reborn when he brought love into my life and now I have to do the same for him."

Jesus offered her an understanding smile. "He'll come around, Di."

She nodded and glanced out the window as they continued the drive in silence. The alley where the Blood Bank was located was too narrow for cars, so they parked by the mouth of the alley and hurried to the door.

Even with the late hour there were nearly two dozen or more people waiting to get in.

Humans, Diana noted from the lack of power drifting off them.

As the bouncer saw them, he smiled and opened the door, earning assorted grumblings and complaints from those on the line until he said, "Shut the fuck up or you won't ever get in."

And that was the epitome of the Blood Bank, Diana thought with a chuckle.

It was crowded inside with a mix of humans and vampires of all ages. No elders, a goodly assortment of undead, and thankfully only a few fledglings. The newly turned were the worst for a number of reasons, from blood urges they found hard to control to cockiness at their new powers.

Never a good mix, Diana thought as Jesus and she approached Foley, who was bartending. All of the stools were taken and waitresses called out orders before flitting back and forth from the bar to the various patrons.

As they reached the bar, Foley grinned and said to the two men sitting in front of him, "Go get yourselves a table and the next round's on me."

Tempted by that offer, the two scooted off and she and Jesus took their spots.

Foley called out to a second vampire bartender that he was taking a break and turned his full attention to them.

"You're looking radiant as usual," Foley said and slapped some cocktail napkins on the counter in front of them.

Diana waved him off as he placed glasses on the napkins. "This isn't a social call, Daniel."

He grasped his hands and clutched them over his chest theatrically. "I'm heartbroken, Di."

She controlled her chuckle and shook her head. "Get serious, please."

"Yes, sir, Special Agent. So what can I do for you?" he said and glanced between her and Jesus.

"Ryder tells us you've got security cameras here," Jesus said.

Foley nodded and motioned to a far point in the club and the camera in the corner. "A couple in here and one outside. Put them in after that nastiness with the slayer's brother slicing and dicing up my waitress."

"Do you think we could get a copy of the outside video feed from earlier tonight?" Jesus asked.

Daniel's brow furrowed and all hints of playfulness left him. "Is something up?"

Jesus hesitated and looked toward her. Obviously he thought it was for her to say.

"Ryder was here earlier, right?"

"Yeah, he was. Popped me. Twice. It was good to see him finally having some spirit," Foley said and rubbed at his jaw, although there wasn't a hint of any damage there.

"Spirit? Maybe if he'd shown a little less spirit we wouldn't have to be here, losing sleep and worrying," she shot back, angry about his almost cavalier attitude.

"He's a vampire. It's in his nature to fight and bite. Or would you rather that he was fangless? Moping around like some kind of neutered pet?" Foley said, and a bit of neon crept into his gaze. Emotion was eroding his control and she understood. At one time Foley had been controlled by someone else, fangless to some extent.

She covered his hand with hers. "I know you fought when you needed to, but this wasn't the time to pick a fight with the slayers."

"The slayers, huh? Yeah, probably not wise with all that's happened lately," he said and jerked his head in the direction of a door to one side of the bar. "The video system is in the back. Give me a second to make a copy of the file."

He rushed into the room and Diana swiveled on the stool to face her friend and boss. His face showed no emotion, but hers must have since he said, "Don't worry, Di. I have no doubt we'll alibi Ryder."

With a sigh, she said, "Yeah, I know. But like I told you during the drive down, it's about more than that."

"I get it, Di, but you're not alone. You've got all of us to lean on."

She gave a small smile, well aware that she had quite a few friends, new and old, mortal and undead, who would have her back.

"When we can drop Ryder from the list of suspects, we'll still have to solve Richard's murder. Especially if it looks like a vampire did it."

Before Jesus could reply, Foley exited the back room and slapped a thumb drive on the counter. "Here it is. I hope it gets you what you need."

"Thank you, Daniel," she said and leaned across the bar to give him a quick hug.

"You'll keep me posted on anything that's happening?" he asked.

"We will. Just keep your eyes open for anything weird."

Foley chuckled and motioned to the patrons of the bar, most of whom qualified for that kind of scrutiny. "Anything weirder than this and it's probably the end of the world."

She said nothing since she didn't think an apocalypse was imminent, but as she walked away, she thought, *Please let it not be the end of my world.*

Chapter 11

The two slayer novitiates at the door of the crematorium chamber moved shoulder-to-shoulder to block their way.

Ben glared at them. "Do you know who we are?"

One of the young men raised his chin a defiant inch and said, "A former elder."

The one next to him tightened his hold on the grip of the short sword at his side and eyed Michaela. Muttering the word as if they were a curse, he said, "And his dhampir whore."

With startling speed, Michaela had a dagger at his throat. The sharp edge of her knife cut his skin like a scalpel and a fine line of blood leaked from the deepest part of the wound.

"Not former and not whore. Council members and don't you forget that," she warned the upstart.

"Open the door. *Now*," Ben said, his tone brooking no disobedience.

The one novitiate stepped aside immediately, but the other one hesitated until Michaela applied a little more pressure and a little more blood was spilled. Enough for him to finally do an awkward and careful step to the side to avoid any more damage to his throat.

Michaela whipped the dagger back, but held it at the ready just in case either of the two had a change of heart, although given their lack of slayer power and training, Michaela and he could deal with them easily.

He hoped that whoever was on the other side of the door could be handled similarly.

As they entered, he took note of two other novitiates standing guard at either side of the gurney holding Richard's body as well as Anthony and Graham, one of the more quiet and usually more reasonable of the slayer elders. They were just about to start stripping Richard to prepare him for the slayer's death rites, but paused as Michaela and he entered.

"What are doing here?" Anthony demanded and walked back around the gurney to block their path to Richard's body.

"The Council charged us with finding out who murdered Richard. Since you didn't let our FBI friends take a look at the body before, we're here to rectify that mistake," Ben said.

Anthony tucked his arms across his chest and with a smug smile said, "Do you really think you'll find anything that exonerates your undead friend?"

"You never know until you look," Michaela said and jerked her head in the direction of the two novitiates and Graham. "Will you honor Richard?" she asked, commencing the start of the ritual.

The trio approached Richard while Michaela and he stood before the body, ready to inspect it. Graham was one of the lesser elders and in other times, he likely would have never been chosen for the Council. But with his own death and Aja's, who had trusted his brother and paid for it with her life, the Council had had to boost their numbers. Even the two novitiates attending the rites were fairly new.

The one, a mixed race girl named Rhiannon, had caught his eye months ago. Not only was she a stunning beauty, but she had natural grace, instincts, and power. She had quickly been moving up the ranks months earlier and she had been assigned to him shortly before his own death and turning. She had been re-assigned to Richard, but with his passing, she was orphaned again.

As her hazel-green gaze connected with his for a moment, he thought he detected pity there as it roved over the ridges and scars left by his brother's attack. Pity was the last thing he wanted to see in that gaze, but he'd leave that – and her – for another time.

In soft and patient tones, Graham directed the two slayers-in-training on handling Richard's body and what the next steps would be. A ritual cleansing of his body with holy water and blessing with fragrant oils. The laying on of hands by those in attendance who, if they were lucky, might be gifted with a touch of his slayer power. Finally, the presentment of a cross atop his body before he was incinerated.

The male novitiate lifted Richard's upper body so that Rhiannon could strip off his shirt. As she did so, the very visible hand prints on his arms, along with the bruising, cuts, and burns from the Taser blasts, became visible to all in the room.

Graham released a sharp gasp and urged the two novitiates away from the body. "This isn't possible," he whispered as he bent to examine the hand prints.

"No vampire did that, Anthony," he said and pointed at the marks.

The arrogant slayer sauntered over and examined Richard's body. "Not unless they were familiar with the dark arts," he challenged.

Michaela released a harsh breath. "Really, Anthony. Tell me something. How familiar are you with them? Or any of the other slayers? These arts were forbidden millennia ago. Only a slayer with intense knowledge of our past would be capable of this."

"Or a vampire who had stolen Richard's journal. Or had a slayer willing to share our secrets with them," Anthony said pointedly and shot a look at him.

"I shared our history and nothing more because I do not know anything more. That's why Ryder and I came to see Richard. To see if he could explain what was happening to Ryder."

Anthony laughed out loud. "That old fairy tale about becoming human again?"

Ben swept his hand across Richard's body. "Maybe it is a fairy tale, but this, what happened to Richard, wasn't about some vamp trying to become human again. This was done by someone with far more power than even a vampire elder would have."

"You're saying it was one of the Council members?" Rhiannon said, earning a glare from Anthony.

"Silence, Rhiannon. You have not yet earned the right to speak before us," Anthony said.

She dipped her head with reverence, but Ben could detect her anger. She had spirit, but also common sense. That was a good combination for a slayer. Now that she'd been orphaned by Richard's death, he'd have to claim her as his trainee at the next Council meeting. Maybe with his influence, she'd become a much more reasonable slayer than the likes of Anthony. He pushed that thought away and returned to the reason they were here.

"We'd like to take some photos of the wounds. Maybe they will assist in tracking down who did this," he said and although Anthony seemed ready to protest it, Graham beat him to the punch.

"Proceed, Benjamin. Anything that will identify who did this would be welcome."

Together, Michaela and he quickly snapped off some photos with her smartphone, making sure to take various angles of Richard's throat, chest, and most importantly, the markings on his arms.

Ben had no doubt that a vampire had not done that theft of power. He was well familiar with all the elders on the Vampire Council and he didn't think that any of them possessed the kind of power needed to overwhelm and drain someone like Richard. Or at least, not unless they had somehow discovered the slayer's dark arts and become masters of it.

But even more troubling was the prospect that a fellow elder was capable of such a deed.

After Michaela and he finished, they stepped aside to allow the other slayers to complete the ritual. Carefully they cleansed Richard's body and anointed him with the fragrant oils, respectfully spreading the oil across his forehead, hands, feet and then the area above his heart while Anthony chanted a sacred prayer, eyes closed and hands outspread.

Soon the aromas of sandalwood, frankincense, myrrh and patchouli filled the air.

The two slayers took up spots at Richard's head and feet while the novitiates stood at either side of him.

Anthony looked around and satisfied that everyone was in place, he said, "Place your hands on Richard at the spots where we have blessed him."

The three did as they were told and once again Anthony closed his eyes and offered up a slayer's prayer, but after the first few verses, the tension in Anthony's voice was impossible to miss.

He stopped mid-verse and shook his head. "The font within him is dry."

Ben recalled Nemesis's words from earlier that night. *Zapped. Wiped clean.*

He repeated his earlier warning. "No vampire did this, Anthony. We'll confirm where Ryder and I were tonight, but you need to warn the Slayer Council – "

"About what, Ben? You're quick to clear your new friends of any hand in this, but I'm sure it's not as impossible as you say."

He was tired of fighting with the other man. "Do what you wish. You'll have the proof of our innocence soon enough."

Michaela jumped in with her own warning. "I just hope that proof isn't another dead slayer, Anthony."

* * *

Diana fast-forwarded through the video from the Blood Bank and did some screen shots confirming Ryder's entry and exit from the vampire club.

After printing them, she turned her attention to the video feeds that Helene and Miguel had taken from an ATM camera on First Avenue and the CCTV feed from one of the traffic cameras. As she had done before, she did screen shots and printed the materials.

Both confirmed Ryder's whereabouts and the timing of them made it virtually impossible for Ryder to have been at Richard's apartment at the time of his death.

She added those screen shots to the ones she already had from the condo's cameras which showed Ben's entrance into the building. Like Ryder, his alibi was looking solid.

Michaela had messaged her the photos they had snapped before Richard was cremated. The hand prints on Richard's arms were very similar to those on Ryder, only these looked much more pronounced, almost like they had been burned into the dead slayer's skin.

The size was different as well, judging from the photos. The pattern was larger, with a more pronounced hand print in the center as if that was the initial point of contact. From there the edges leaked outward like a tie dyed design.

She hoped Maggie, her best friend and the FBI's Forensics expert, could make sense of it as well as the photos of the blood patterns. With it being a full moon, she and David were still in their shifter forms and roaming the night, but in a couple of hours, they'd be back to being human and at work down at the FBI's headquarters in Federal Plaza.

Satisfied with the new information she had just received, she exited her office and marched to the living room where Ben, Michaela, Jesus, and Ryder all waited for her.

Michaela was tucked against Jesus on the couch. Ben was across from them in one of the comfy leather chairs. Ryder was on his feet, pacing back and forth anxiously before the wall of windows leading out onto their balcony. He whirled around as she came back in, the look on his face expectant, but also troubled.

She held the papers up and said, "We've got enough to dispel the Slayer Council's allegations that either you or Ben were somehow involved with Richard's death."

The tension in Ryder's body dissipated, but didn't totally leave. He stalked over to the group and stood there, fists clenched at his sides. "But what you have doesn't tell us who killed Richard."

She shook her head. "No, it doesn't, but it does point the investigation toward someone connected with the slayers."

"Not necessarily," Ben said and shot a worried look at Michaela.

"What do you mean by that?" Ryder asked.

With a shrug, Michaela offered up the explanation. "Those wounds on Richard's arms are from the theft of his life energies, including his slayer power. The most likely assailant would be someone with knowledge of the slayers' dark rituals. Rituals that caused the fall from grace of one of the first slayers."

"And which possibly created the first vampire," Ben added.

"So anyone, including a vampire, could have done this?" she asked, just to make sure she was understanding where they were going with their assertions.

"It would have to be a powerful vampire," Michaela said.

Diana didn't fail to miss the glance she gave Ryder from the corner of her eye. A glance that worried her because she needed all of their team on board to handle the slayers.

"And one who somehow had gained access to the slayers' practices which would be hard to do. It's why the slayers terminate those who fail out of their program," Michaela added.

"Very humane," Jesus said and hugged Michaela hard. "It makes me wonder why you ever joined up with them."

"For survival, J. Without what I learned from the slayers, I could never have faced Connall on my own. But I also couldn't have defeated him without all of you," she said with a grateful smile at all of them, Ryder included.

Ryder tensed up again at the mention of Michaela's father, the ancient vampire who had nearly killed him a month earlier. To draw attention away from that, she said, "But we know that termination orders are sometimes not fulfilled, like with your brother, Ben."

"That was a rare occurrence, Diana. And one which cost us dearly," he said.

"How else could someone know the slayers' rites?" Jesus asked and both Michaela and Ben answered at the same time.

"Slayer journals."

Ben quickly added, "Richard was in possession of one of the oldest slayer journals. According to Anthony, it's missing."

"Could this journal have information on those dark rituals you mentioned?" she asked.

Ben nodded. "It was one of the oldest, predating the fall from grace. Because of that, it might contain a number of practices that have since been banned by the Slayer Council."

"So if we find the journal, we may find the killer?" Jesus asked.

"Possibly," Michaela answered.

"Why only possibly?" Diana pressed.

With another shrug, Michaela said, "Because we don't know when the journal was taken. Considering how Richard was killed, it may have been taken before his murder – "

"Because whoever killed him used one of the rituals in the journal," Ryder finished for her.

"I guess we'll deal with that possibility once we know more. For now, will you provide the information about the alibis to the Slayer Council?" she asked Ben and Michaela.

"We will," Michaela said and rose from the couch. "It's time we went home. You've got work in the morning."

"Wouldn't be the first or last time I pull an all nighter," Jesus grumbled.

"I'll be heading out as well. If you need me, you know where I'll be," Ben said and followed the couple out of the apartment.

Diana closed the door and then leaned against it as she stared at her husband.

He hadn't moved from his spot. It was painfully obvious from his posture and from the upset she sensed in him through the connection they shared that he was still very troubled.

"Talk to me, Ryder."

With a massive hunch of his shoulders, he looked down and said, "What's there to talk about?"

She shoved away from the door and stalked to him. Positioned herself so that there was no way he could avoid looking at her. "Don't shut me out, Ryder. Please don't shut me out."

He blew out an exasperated breath and wagged his head. "You saw the look Michaela gave me. She's still not one hundred percent sure that I didn't have anything to do with Richard's death."

"But we both know that you didn't. In time she will as well."

Ryder wanted to believe his wife. Wanted to believe that everything would be all right with the slayers, but he couldn't. "The slayers won't stop until they know who killed Richard."

Diana cupped his cheek and gazed at him lovingly. "We won't either, Ryder."

"This isn't the life I wanted for us. For Charlie. Always fighting. Always hoping just to make it just another day."

"Tomorrow is promised to no one. Isn't that the old adage?" she said and wrapped her arms around him, hugging him hard.

Except that vampires and dhampirs had a wealth of tomorrows. Did he still have them or were the changes in his body signaling that his tomorrows were growing shorter in number?

"Not sure they were thinking about vampires when they coined that phrase," he said as the peace of her embrace seeped into him, providing comfort and driving away his fears.

A light laugh escaped her. She tilted her head up and met his gaze. "Life isn't easy, especially for people like us."

"Now, it isn't, but I will fight for us, darlin'. I will keep you and Charlie safe."

"But you don't have to fight alone, Ryder. The past month you've been so distant. Shouldering the burden yourself, but I'm here, Ryder," she said and tapped her chest. "I'm here to stand beside you. Be your wing man no matter what happens."

He couldn't resist her earnestness or baiting her a bit. "My wing man, huh? I think I can handle that."

An almost effervescent smile transformed her face. "What else can you handle?" she teased sexily and smoothed her hand across his chest.

He was about to answer when a knock came at their front door. Considering it was almost three in the morning it was totally unexpected. He immediately worried that something was wrong with Charlie, who Melissa and Sebastian had agreed to watch until the morning.

Together they walked to the door and he peered through the peephole to find Jason, his doorman, waiting outside.

He flung open the door and the young vampire held out a small package that was crudely wrapped in kraft paper and twine.

"A courier brought this by and I was heading for a break so I thought I'd bring it up myself."

"A courier at this hour of the night?" Diana asked.

Jason shrugged. "Yeah, I kind of thought it was weird myself. Not your typical time for drop offs, but he said it was a priority delivery."

Ryder accepted the package and immediately experienced an almost electrical charge across his palms.

"Which delivery company left this again?" he asked and narrowed his gaze at he looked at the package, which bore no written address or other markings.

"Not the brown company or one of the other regulars. It was a bike courier. Rode up, left it with me, and then took off. I didn't even really get a good look at him," Jason said.

He met his wife's gaze and it was plainly obvious she was as concerned as he was.

"Thanks, Jason. We appreciate you bringing it up right away," he said, reached into his pocket and offered the young man a tip, which he refused.

"No way, Ryder. You just gave me an awesome raise last month, remember?" he said and walked toward the elevator.

He'd gotten the raise because the vampire who'd almost beaten Ryder to death had also carved up Jason pretty badly, but the young vampire had held his ground. It was the least he could do to reward his loyalty.

Closing the door, he turned and walked with the package to the couch and after Diana was sitting beside him, he placed it on the coffee table and undid the twine. The kraft paper beneath wasn't secured by tape or glue and immediately came loose.

He pulled aside the paper to reveal the leather-bound journal inside. Roughly six by nine, it was at least three thick inches of parchment paper and judging from the looks of both the cover and paper, quite old. It was clear from the patina on the cover that the journal had been handled often. It had the rich look of both age and tender care.

Much like with the package, there were no external markings on the cover to give a hint as to what was within, not that he needed the hint.

"Is that what I think it is?" Diana asked and skimmed a finger across the cover, quickly recoiling from that simple touch. "What the hell was that?"

He glanced at her. "You felt it, too? Like an electrical charge?"

She nodded and reached for it again, more cautiously. Gingerly she flipped open the cover to reveal the inscription inside.

"Great. It's in Latin," she said.

"A required language in my day," he replied and translated for her. "Aurelius Magnus, Chief Slayer of Rome. May all who read this guard our secrets upon the threat of death."

"This must be the journal Richard had. The one stolen from his apartment."

"Yeah, it has to be that one, darlin'," he said and skimmed through the first few pages, experiencing the seepage of power from the journal with each touch. It had been a long time since he'd read in Latin, but he remembered enough bits and pieces to understand that the journal not only contained stories about the history of the slayers but also a number of rituals.

He'd bet that there were instructions for the dark arts practiced on Richard in the journal as well.

He also had no doubt about something else. "They want a reason to kill us."

Diana nodded. "Yeah, they do, only we have proof of when this was delivered."

"I'll have Sam send up a copy of the video recordings for the last hour. But what do we do about this in the meantime?" he asked and held the book out to her.

She accepted it gingerly and stared at the cover for a long moment. Lifting her gaze to his, she said, "We read it. Find out if it says anything about what's happening to you. Find out if it has whatever spells or rites were used on Richard."

"The Slayer Council is going to mightily pissed off if we don't give it back right away."

She grinned, but then her look turned serious. She laid a hand on his chest and said, "Yeah, I know. But this is important to you. To us."

Ryder smiled. "It is, darlin'. And we'll figure this out. We always do."

She smiled again, rose up on tiptoe and kissed him. He wrapped his arms around her and kept her close, the slayer's journal tucked between them. It warmed and vibrated against them before they reluctantly ended the embrace.

"We need to secure this and then get some rest. It'll be morning soon and time for us to pick up Charlie," she said.

"I'll put it in the safe in my office." Together they walked up to his office where they locked the journal away.

After, they crossed the hall to their bedroom where they undressed quickly and slipped into bed.

As he lay on his back, Diana tucked herself into his side and skimmed her hand across his chest in a lazy back and forth motion. She sighed and propped her head up on her hand to look at him.

"They're going to do everything they can to get that journal back. You know that, don't you?"

He brushed his thumb along her cheekbone. "I know, but it's worth the battle, isn't it?"

With a small smile, she nodded and said, "Our love, our family, is worth the fight, Ryder."

He captured the smile on her lips with his own, bringing his mouth to hers and kissing her. Whispering against her lips, "I will always fight for you. For Charlie."

She answered him by deepening the kiss and covering his body with hers. Taking him inside her.

"I love you, Ryder," she said and wrapped her arms around him.

"I love you, too," he said and as he let her love draw him in, it brought him the peace he had lacked for so long.

A peace that he'd fight for with every beat of his undead heart.

*　*　*

Look for FIGHT FOR LOVE, the continuation of Diana and Ryder's story

and a new romance for Ben, in Early Summer 2014.

❧ THE END ❧

About the Author

Caridad Pineiro is a New York Times and USA Today bestselling author and RITA® Finalist. Caridad wrote her first novel in the fifth grade when her teacher assigned a project – to write a book for a class lending library. Bitten by the writing bug, Caridad continued with her passion for the written word and in 1999, Caridad's first novel was released. Over a decade later, Caridad is the author of nearly 40 published novels and novellas. When not writing, Caridad is a wife, and mother to an aspiring writer and fashionista. For more information, please visit www.caridad.com or rebornvampirenovels.com.

Follow Charity on Twitter at https://twitter.com/caridadpineiro and on Facebook at https://www.facebook.com/Caridad.Author.

Additional Books by the Author Writing as Charity Pineiro

NOW AND ALWAYS June 2013 ISBN 1490362770
FAITH IN YOU July 2013 ISBN 1490412697
TORI GOT LUCKY December 2013 ISBN 1494775182
THE PERFECT MIX March 2014 1495948234

Additional Books by the Author Writing as Caridad Pineiro

Books in The Gambling for Love Romantic Suspense Series

THE PRINCE'S GAMBLE November 2012 ISBN 9781622668007 Entangled Publishing
TO CATCH A PRINCESS August 2013 ISBN 9781622661329 Entangled Publishing

Books in The Sin Hunter Paranormal Romance Series

THE CLAIMED May 2012 ISBN 978-0446584609 Forever Grand Central Publishing
THE LOST August 2011 ISBN 978-0446584616 Forever Grand Central Publishing

Books in The Sins Paranormal Romance Series

STRONGER THAN SIN November 2010 ISBN 0446543845 Forever Grand Central Publishing
SINS OF THE FLESH November 2009 ISBN 0446543837 Forever Grand Central Publishing

Other Novels by Caridad

THE FIFTH KINDOM July 2011 ISBN 9781426891885 Carina Press
SOLDIER'S SECRET CHILD Dec 2008 ISBN 0373276109 Silhouette Romantic Suspense

Novellas

GHOST OF A CHANCE, paranormal short story November 2012 ISBN B00AUGV89G Caridad Pineiro Publishing
HER VAMPIRE LOVER October 2012 ISBN 9781459242289 Nocturne Cravings Novella
NIGHT OF THE COUGAR June 2012 ISBN 9781459231153 Nocturne Cravings Novella
THE VAMPIRE'S CONSORT April 2012 ISBN 9781459222731 Harlequin Nocturne Cravings Novella
NOCTURNAL WHISPERS February 2012 ISBN 9781459221437 Harlequin Nocturne Cravings Novella
AMAZON AWAKENING December 2011 ISBN 9781459282766 Available Harlequin Nocturne Cravings Novella
WHEN HERALD ANGELS SING novella in A VAMPIRE FOR CHRISTMAS October 2011 ISBN 0373776446 HQN
AZTEC GOLD January 2011 ISBN 9781426891045 Carina Press Novella
Crazy for the Cat in MOON FEVER Oct 2007 ISBN 1416514902 Pocket Books

Books in THE CALLING/THE REBORN Vampire Novel Series

DIE FOR LOVE, December 2013, ASIN B00H6EFD5U Entangled Publishing
BORN TO LOVE, November 2013, ISBN 9781622663705 Entangled Publishing
TO LOVE OR SERVE, October 2013, ISBN 9781622663477Entangled Publishing
FOR LOVE OR VENGEANCE September 2013 ISBN 9781622662937 Entangled Publishing
KISSED BY A VAMPIRE (formerly ARDOR CALLS) October 2012 ISBN 9780373885589 Harlequin Nocturne
AWAKENING THE BEAST Collection featuring HONOR CALLS October 2009 ISBN 0373250940 Silhouette Nocturne
FURY CALLS March 2009 ISBN 0373618077 Silhouette Nocturne
HONOR CALLS February 2009 ISBN 9781426828362 Nocturne Bite
HOLIDAY WITH A VAMPIRE December 2007 ISBN 0373617763 Silhouette Nocturne
THE CALLING COMPLETE COLLECTION October 2008 ISBN 9781426807657 Silhouette Includes Darkness Calls, Danger Calls,

Temptation Calls, Death Calls, Devotion Calls, and Blood Calls–as well as a the online read Desire Calls.
BLOOD CALLS May 2007 ISBN 0373617631 Silhouette Nocturne
DEVOTION CALLS January 2007 ISBN 0373617550 Silhouette Nocturne
DEATH CALLS Dec 2006 ISBN 0373617534 Silhouette Nocturne
TEMPTATION CALLS Oct 2005 ISBN 0373274602 Silhouette Intimate Moments
DANGER CALLS June 2005 ISBN 0373274416 Silhouette Intimate Moments
DARKNESS CALLS Mar 2004 ISBN 0373273533 Silhouette Intimate Moments

Romantic Suspense Series

SECRET AGENT REUNION Aug 2007 ISBN 0373275463 Silhouette Romantic Suspense
MORE THAN A MISSION Aug 2006 ISBN 037327498X Silhouette Intimate Moments

Printed in Great Britain
by Amazon